Dear Reader,

When I first started writing, I didn't understand the magic that happens with certain characters and situations. They can take on a life of their own. That certainly happened with the four Randall brothers I created in the series BRIDES FOR BROTHERS. I fell in love with these men, and I was gratified when some of you let me know you did too.

Now I'm asking you to come back with me to the Randall spread in Wyoming to see what happened to B.J.'s son, Toby, a Randall by adoption. I know it hasn't been long enough, but I knew his story by the time I finished Jake's book, and I couldn't wait any longer.

Along with Toby, there are a lot of members of the Randall family in the second generation. Jake's matchmaking really paid off. More Randall stories are banging on my door, anxious to come alive. As you can see, I have a lot of plans!

The editors wold love to know what you think about the Randall family. You can write to them at:

Harlequin Books—Dept AW
300 East 42nd Street, 6th Floor
New York, NY 10017

I hope we can meet at the Randall spread often in the future!

Judy Christenberry

Dear Reader,

Welcome to another month of wonderful books from Harlequin American Romance. We've rounded up the best stories by your favorite authors for you to enjoy.

Bestselling author Judy Christenberry brings readers a new generation of her popular Randall family as she returns to her BRIDES FOR BROTHERS series. Sweet Elizabeth is about to marry another man, and rodeo star Toby Randall will let nothing stand in the way of him stopping her wedding. Don't miss *Randall Pride*.

An injured firefighter and the woman he rescued in an earthquake learn about the healing power of love in Charlotte Maclay's latest novel, *Bold and Brave-Hearted*. This is the first book of her exciting new miniseries MEN OF STATION SIX. In *Twins Times Two!* by Lisa Bingham, a single mom agrees to a marriage in name only to a handsome single dad in order to keep together their two sets of twins, who were separated at birth. And enemies are forced to become Mr. and Mrs. in *Court-Appointed Marriage* by Dianne Castell, part of Harlequin American Romance's theme promotion THE WAY WE MET...AND MARRIED.

Enjoy this month's offerings, and make sure to return each and every month to Harlequin American Romance!

Wishing you happy reading,

Melissa Jeglinski
Associate Senior Editor
Harlequin American Romance

⑥

Judy Christenberry

Randall Pride

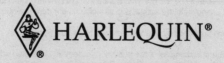

TORONTO • NEW YORK • LONDON
AMSTERDAM • PARIS • SYDNEY • HAMBURG
STOCKHOLM • ATHENS • TOKYO • MILAN • MADRID
PRAGUE • WARSAW • BUDAPEST • AUCKLAND

ISBN 0-373-16885-3

RANDALL PRIDE

This edition published by arrangement with Harlequin Books S.A.

Visit us at www.eHarlequin.com

Printed in U.S.A.

ABOUT THE AUTHOR

Judy Christenberry has been writing romances for fifteen years because she loves happy endings as much as her readers. A former French teacher, Judy now devotes herself to writing full-time. She hopes readers have as much fun reading her stories as she does writing them. She spends her spare time reading, watching her favorite sports teams and keeping track of her two daughters. Judy's a native Texan, but now lives in Arizona.

Books by Judy Christenberry

HARLEQUIN AMERICAN ROMANCE

555—FINDING DADDY
579—WHO'S THE DADDY?
612—WANTED: CHRISTMAS MOMMY
626—DADDY ON DEMAND
649—COWBOY CUPID*
653—COWBOY DADDY*
661—COWBOY GROOM*
665—COWBOY SURRENDER*
701—IN PAPA BEAR'S BED
726—A COWBOY AT HEART
735—MY DADDY THE DUKE
744—COWBOY COME HOME*
755—COWBOY SANTA
773—ONE HOT DADDY-TO-BE?†
777—SURPRISE—YOU'RE A DADDY!†
781—DADDY UNKNOWN†
785—THE LAST STUBBORN COWBOY†
802—BABY 2000
817—THE GREAT TEXAS WEDDING BARGAIN†
842—THE $10,000,000 TEXAS WEDDING†
853—PATCHWORK FAMILY
867—RENT A MILLIONAIRE GROOM
878—STRUCK BY THE TEXAS MATCHMAKERS†
885—RANDALL PRIDE*

*Brides for Brothers
†Tots for Texans

THE RANDALLS

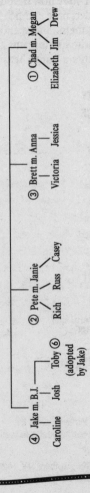

④ Jake m. B.J.

Caroline   Josh   Toby ⑥
                  (adopted
                   by Jake)

② Pete m. Janie

Rich   Russ   Casey

③ Brett m. Anna

Victoria   Jessica

① Chad m. Megan

Elizabeth   Jim   Drew

⑤ Griffin m. Camille   (stepsister to Megan)
   (cousin)
              John

           Melissa

① Cowboy Cupid
② Cowboy Daddy
③ Cowboy Groom
④ Cowboy Surrender
⑤ Cowboy Come Home
⑥ Randall Pride

Chapter One

Toby Randall drew a deep breath as the huge house came into view. Home. Like the man without a country, Toby felt as if he'd finally been pardoned.

He hadn't told his parents he was coming. Or even more importantly, that he wanted to stay…if he could.

When he'd received that last e-mail from his mother Sunday afternoon, she'd passed on the Randall family news, as usual. It had only taken one sentence to change the direction of his life.

A shout brought him out of his thoughts.

"Toby!"

He recognized his baby brother Josh's voice from telephone calls home. But the gangly figure jumping up and down must've grown a foot since he'd last seen him.

Toby waved through the open window. After waving back, Josh turned and sprinted for the house.

By the time Toby had parked, his mother, B.J., met him at the back of his rig, throwing her arms around his neck. "Toby! You didn't tell us you were coming,'' B.J. protested. Since his mother had cut back her hours as a vet when she was pregnant with Josh eighteen years ago, he'd figured she'd be home. It would give him time to visit with her and Aunt Mildred before his dad got home.

"Hi, Mom. Thought I'd surprise you."

"I'm so glad you did. How long can you stay? Where's your next rodeo?" She was patting his cheeks, tears in her eyes.

He knew his travels upset her and Mildred. He knew she'd be happy for him to stay here. But she wasn't the reason he'd stayed away. He hadn't been ready to explain himself. He hoped he wouldn't have to now.

"I'm taking a little break," he muttered, hugging her even closer. "Where's Aunt Mildred?"

"She and Red are taking their afternoon siesta."

When he, his mom and Aunt Mildred had moved to the Randall ranch twenty-three years ago, Mildred had taken on the role of housekeeper—or assistant housekeeper to Red, the cowboy who took care of the four Randall bachelors. Toby couldn't imagine those two being anywhere else, especially since they'd married. They'd also played the role of grandparents to all the Randalls…and him.

B.J. linked her arm with his and began tugging him toward the house.

"Mom, I've got to unload my horses."

"Oh. Of course. I'll help you. Any injuries?"

'Cocoa got kicked by a mangy steer, but I think he's healing all right.''

The two of them unloaded the geldings, and B.J. was feeling Cocoa's leg when the back door slammed open and Mildred and Red, followed by Josh, spilled out of the house. "Hey, what's Josh doing at home?" Toby suddenly asked. "Hasn't school started yet?"

"No. He's in college now, you know, or will be. He'd be out with your dad, but he's getting over the flu. I'm making him take it easy one more day."

By the time B.J. finished explaining, Red and Mildred swept him into a group hug and plied him with questions as his mother had.

"I called Dad!" Josh announced. "He's on his way."

"You shouldn't have interrupted his work," Toby protested.

"Ha!" B.J. snapped, with a grin. "If Josh hadn't called him, I would. You know he complains when he doesn't get as much time with you as we do."

Toby gave silent thanks for the father who'd raised him—Jake Randall. He never made Toby feel like a second-class Randall. The two of them—Jake, thirty-five, and Toby, four—had become friends at once. The first thing Jake had done after marrying his mom had been to adopt Toby.

He cleared his throat, afraid someone would notice the tears in his eyes. Damn, it was good to be home.

AFTER PUTTING his horses in a corral where they could move around after having been in the trailer since five that morning, Toby followed the others into the big kitchen where he'd spent much of his life. Mildred immediately poured him a cup of freshly made coffee and added a plate of her cookies. He'd loved those cookies as a child, and he still did.

With a casual shrug of his shoulders, Toby asked, "Where is everyone?"

"Aren't we enough?" Red asked, a teasing glint in his eyes.

"Sure," Toby said heartily, hoping no one noticed his consternation, and took a big gulp of coffee.

"Your sister is already back in Laramie at school. It's her senior year," his mother said, taking pity on him. "You remember Caroline has decided to get a medical degree? She and Victoria and Jessica went down early to redecorate their apartment. And Lizzie is out. The twins and Jim are with the guys getting some work done. Jim and Josh are going down to Laramie this weekend. Drew and Casey are in class." She looked at Red. "Did I forget anyone?"

"Nope," Red said, frowning. "I think that covers all the cousins. Nary a baby among them."

"You mean Casey counts as an adult now?" Toby teased.

"Well, we're making him use training wheels," Red said with a big grin.

Mildred added, "Your aunts are all at work."

"Janie's out with the guys?" His uncle Pete's wife, Janie, had been raised on a ranch and pitched in when they needed an extra hand. "You must be short-handed right now," Toby said, holding his breath for the answer.

"Actually, we are," B.J said. "But Janie's not here. I told you her father died, didn't I? She—and Pete—are spending a lot of time over there, when they can be spared."

Toby let out the breath he'd been holding. He'd been afraid they wouldn't need his help. "Is good help as hard to find as it usually is?"

Red stared at him. "*Good* help is always hard to find. Too many boys want the glamour of the rodeo."

Mildred elbowed him.

When Toby had chosen the rodeo life, his parents had let him go without complaint. But he'd known it wasn't what they wanted for him.

He hadn't had a choice.

Before he could say anything, they heard boots racing toward the house.

Toby jumped to his feet and ran out to the porch, his gaze eagerly searching for Jake.

"Dad!" he cried and the two men met in a rough embrace.

"'Bout time you got home, son!" Jake scolded.

"I know, Dad."

Jake wrapped an arm around Toby's shoulders and started into the house.

"Hey! Don't we get a hug?" Pete called.

Toby turned and greeted his three uncles, Pete, Brett and Chad, and then his cousins, before they all entered the house. His cousins left to shower before dinner, telling him they'd catch him later. They couldn't ask their questions about the rodeo scene, buckle bunnies and all, in front of the women.

Toby always downplayed the glamorous part of rodeoing. He didn't want his cousins out on the circuit.

The men of the family sat down with coffee and cookies.

"How long can you stay?" Jake asked.

"He said he's taking a break," B.J. answered for him, a big smile on her face.

Toby cleared his throat as his father continued to stare at him. "Actually, I was wondering...Red said you were thinking about hiring some more help. I wondered if I'd do?"

Stark silence fell around the room. Toby had done well in rodeo. He'd won Cowboy of the Year at Nationals twice. His winnings had provided much more than a nest egg. He could buy his own ranch now. In addition, he'd done a number of ads for jean companies, boot- and hat-makers, and would still be in demand for a number of years, even if he retired today.

He'd realized his request would surprise them, but he'd hoped they would welcome him.

He filled the awkward silence. "If you don't think I'd be of any use—"

Before he could finish Jake shoved back his chair and pulled Toby into another hug. "Damn it, what do you mean be of any use? Of course we want you, son.''

Since his uncles were just as enthusiastic, the questions Toby had melted away.

He'd finally come home.

BEFORE DINNER, Toby stood on the back porch with his cousins and little brother. The next generation of Randall males were questioning Toby about the lifestyle he was abandoning.

"Man, I can't believe you're giving up all that money. And the ladies," Russ, one of the twins, said. "'Course, you'll be a legend for a while, but—''

"It's pretty tiring being a legend," Toby said. "I missed being at home with you guys. And Mom and Dad.''

"You're crazy," Rich, the other twin, exclaimed. "We work like dogs.''

"It's good, honest work," Toby said, smiling. He understood the attraction of making a name for yourself. But he'd been there, done that.

"But what about—" Josh, his brother, began, but he stopped when he heard a car coming from the road. "Damn, that's got to be Lizzie and that city dude she's going to marry." The disgust in his voice was clear to everyone.

Toby froze, his attention on the car topping the hill now. But he took note of the others' attitudes.

"Yeah," Jim, Elizabeth's younger brother added,

"I can't believe my own sister would choose a jerk like him."

Toby looked at the twins, the oldest in the group, but there was no anticipation on their faces.

What kind of man had Elizabeth chosen?

The car pulled to a halt and the passenger door opened. Elizabeth Randall stepped out of the car. His cousin in everything but blood.

Toby stopped breathing as the slim, auburn-haired young woman appeared. Elizabeth had always been beautiful. As a child, her delicate features and glowing skin had drawn attention. But grown up, with a woman's body, hair halfway down her back, she was stunning.

He drew in a deep breath.

Elizabeth eyed her brothers and cousins as she waited for her escort, until she caught sight of Toby. With a shriek of joy, she ran straight for him. His arms automatically reached to catch her, and he found himself holding her tightly as she rained kisses on his face.

Heaven and hell.

ELIZABETH was almost as surprised by the rush of emotion she felt at seeing Toby back home as anyone else. She'd scarcely seen him since before she left for college. Somehow, her trips home had not coincided with his rare visits. But she'd worshipped him as a little girl. Five years older, Toby had seemed all-knowing. And he'd been her protector. Hers and Caroline's. Even her brothers and cousins knew better than to pick on either of them, or Toby would find a way to punish them.

That's what it was. She'd missed Toby not being in her life.

"Excuse me, Elizabeth, but who's this man you're hugging?"

The stiff voice belonged to her fiancé. Reluctantly, Elizabeth turned to smile at him. "Sorry, Cleve, but this is my oldest cousin, Toby. I haven't seen him in years."

"Good thing," Cleve muttered even as he extended his hand.

Elizabeth cringed inside. It seemed important to her that Toby approve of her fiancé. No one else in the family did. She'd apologized to Cleve. His superior air, as if his sophistication made everyone jealous, annoyed her. And made her question her choice. But they'd only been engaged twenty-four hours when he'd first met the family. She figured they'd all get along once they got to know each other.

"Kids—" Jake began, opening the back door. Then he started again. "Oh, Mr. O'Banyon, I didn't realize you'd arrived. Elizabeth, you should've brought Mr. O'Banyon through the front door."

Toby looked at her fiancé and realized the man had no idea he'd been insulted. Family, even friends and neighbors, never used the front door.

Instead, Cleve swelled with importance. Then he said, "It's all right, Mr. Randall. I'm sure Elizabeth will remember the next time." Then he added, with disapproval, "She appeared to be excited about this gentleman's arrival."

As if Cleve wouldn't know, Jake wrapped his arm around Toby with a warm smile, and said, "My oldest son."

Cleve stared at the two of them.

"He doesn't look like the rest of you."

Toby said nothing. Their coloring was close, but his eyes were more golden than the warm brown of the rest of the Randalls. Being known as a Randall was the proudest thing in his life. He had worked harder than anyone, been the most accomplished of the Randalls because he'd had the gift of becoming a Randall. He hadn't ever wanted to disappoint Jake. But he knew he really wasn't a Randall.

His family, however, immediately responded to Cleve's comment. They all assured Cleve, in various ways, that Toby was a Randall through and through. It was Elizabeth who ended the protest. She stepped back to Toby's side and wrapped her arm around his waist.

"Toby is part of my family, a very important part."

There was a finality in her voice that told everyone within hearing, even Cleve, how Toby fit in the family. For her efforts, she received a beaming smile from Jake and corroborating nods and grunts from the others.

She didn't receive any appreciation from Toby. He pulled away and moved to the back door. "We don't want to keep the ladies waiting." She supposed it was his excuse for his abrupt movement, but it struck Elizabeth in her heart.

Everyone funneled into the kitchen after him. Elizabeth watched him move to his mother's side, wondering if he'd changed so much in the years he'd been gone. She suddenly remembered the last summer before he'd left for college. She'd caught him kissing a girl at the Fourth of July party. She'd been devastated to see him with his arms around another woman. Her mother had pointed out that he was a young man. She was five years younger, too young to even think about those kinds of activities.

She supposed he'd kissed a lot of women since then.

"Hi, Mom. What's for dinner?" Toby asked.

B.J. kissed him on the cheek. "We changed the menu just for you. Red is making his chicken-fried steak."

As Toby smiled at his mother, someone muttered, "How bourgeois."

Everyone turned to stare at Cleve, and Elizabeth's cheeks flushed.

Red pokered up. "Boy, if you don't like—"

Jake quietly stopped him. "Red, mind sliding a rib eye under the grill? That might be more to Cleve's taste."

Red muttered something under his breath and turned his back on the guest.

Toby tried to search for a distraction. "Hey, you haven't set the table. We'll do it for you."

Mildred shot him a nervous look. "We've already set the table...in the dining room."

Toby realized the reason for Mildred's concern. They never ate in the dining room except at Christmas. They were a boisterous, loving family. Dinner was their opportunity to catch up on everyone's day. Though taught good manners, they all participated in the many conversations flowing around the table.

Toby suspected dinner tonight would be silent and over quickly.

Elizabeth almost pulled Cleve aside then and there and told him their engagement was going to be brief. Like, ending tonight. He might have fit into her life in Laramie, but it was clear Cleve would never be comfortable with her family or vice versa. Her automatic choice came down on her family's side.

Had she ever really loved him? It made her sound fickle. Maybe if she gave it a few more days.

"Elizabeth," her mother, Megan, said. "Why don't you take Cleve into the living room? We'll have everything ready in a few moments."

Elizabeth looked disturbed, and Megan added, "Boys, go with Elizabeth and Cleve. It will give you the chance to get to know him better."

Toby knew he was included in that general direction, but he didn't want to comply. The last thing he wanted to do was get to know Cleve better. He hoped his cousin's engagement would be short, and that they'd move back to Laramie at once.

It was his only hope.

AFTER DINNER, B.J. called her daughter, Caroline, to tell her Toby was moving home. Caroline demanded to speak to her oldest brother.

"Finally!" she greeted him. "I was beginning to think my own brother hated me! I haven't seen you since Christmas. Even then you avoided me."

"Did not, squirt," he returned with a grin. "I was trying not to bully you like you used to accuse me of doing."

"I don't believe you. What's wrong? Did you start losing? Are the women turning you down? Did you get too old?"

"Watch it, brat," he warned his little sister. "When are you coming home?"

"Next Friday. I'm not going to miss a chance to see the famous Toby Randall! My friends will all be so jealous."

"There you go again, showing no respect. No man's going to want a sassy woman."

Her voice changed, turning smooth and silky. "Oh, you'd be surprised, big brother."

"I'm having a talk with you as soon as you get here, little girl," he warned.

"Practice on Elizabeth. Get rid of that jerk she says she's going to marry!"

Toby's breath caught in his throat, and he coughed. "Elizabeth's not my sister, honey," he finally said softly. "It's not my business if she wants to marry him."

She didn't respond, and Toby tried again. "She's—"

Then Caroline found her voice. "What's wrong with you, Toby? When Harry Stiller picked on her in the fifth grade, you fixed him. Why can't you take care of stupid Cleve?"

Toby wanted to hang up. It was a question he didn't have an answer for. "We're all grown up, Caroline. We're allowed to handle our own problems, make our own choices."

"Well, your choices stink!" she snapped. Then she hung up the phone.

He said goodbye to the buzzing in his ear, so his parents wouldn't know Caroline was mad at him.

He stood up, unable to remain in the house; he needed some space to breathe…away from Cleve O'Banyon. He edged toward the door.

"Oh, Toby," B.J. said, "I wanted to talk to Caro. Did she say when she's coming home?"

"Yeah, Friday," he said, hoping she showed up in spite of her anger.

He got out of the room, drawing a relieved breath, until a hand clapped him on the shoulder.

Jake had followed him out of the living room. "Going to check on your horses?"

Toby nodded. That was as good a reason as any he could come up with.

When they reached the barn, Jake didn't look at horseflesh. He turned toward Toby and asked the one question Toby didn't want to answer. "Son, what's wrong?"

Chapter Two

Before Toby could come up with an answer—an answer that wasn't a downright lie, Jake asked another question.

"Have you changed your mind?"

"No, Dad. I'm happy about coming home."

"You won't miss the excitement? I want you to know that if you do, we'll understand." Jake's smile was a little wistful, but as always, he was standing back, letting Toby make his own decisions.

Toby smiled. "I appreciate it, Dad, but the excitement of the rodeo pales next to being at home. I'm glad you and the uncles want me here."

"If it's not that, then what's bothering you?"

Damn, Toby thought he'd distracted Jake. "I'm a little surprised by Elizabeth's choice. But living in Laramie, I guess things are different."

"Not that much," Jake said with a sigh. "But you can join the Cleve O'Banyon Hate Club here on the ranch."

Toby looked at Jake out of the corner of his eye. "Are you a member?"

"Hell, yes. But the president is Chad."

Toby wasn't surprised. Chad, as the youngest of the Randall brothers, had always seemed the most impatient. And Elizabeth was his favorite and only daughter.

"Well, as long as she's happy. I guess Cleve fits in well in Laramie."

Jake turned to stare at him. "But they're not going to live in Laramie."

Toby felt a tremor run through him. "What? Where are they going to live?"

"Here," Jake said succinctly.

"But—but what would they do here?" Toby asked, frantically hoping he'd misunderstood.

"Elizabeth has already begun her job as kindergarten teacher in Rawhide. Classes started two weeks ago. I thought you knew."

Double damn! Toby had thought he'd have some distance from Elizabeth as soon as she married. "But what is Cleve going to do? Let her support him?"

Jake sighed. "No. He's an accountant. He's going to join Bill Johnson's accounting firm. It appears business is growing for Bill. He needs help."

Toby pictured Bill Johnson in his mind. His appearance was that of a "good old boy." He wore jeans to work every day and had never had his hair styled in his life. But his mind was brilliant.

"Has he met Cleve?" Toby asked

Jake grinned. "I know what you're thinking. They don't match, do they? He met him this afternoon. I was dying to ask how it went at dinner, but your mama threatened me."

Toby snorted. His mother didn't throw any fear into her husband. But Jake listened to her good sense. "Good thinking," he agreed.

But while he found the information amusing, it didn't diminish his problem. Of course, they'd live in town and he probably wouldn't see either of them much since he'd be on the ranch. His breath caught in his throat. "They're not—not going to live out here, are they?"

"Hell, no, boy. Prissy-pants wouldn't think of it!" Jake replied, imitating the horror he thought Cleve would show.

Toby laughed. "Where am I going to sleep?" he asked, abruptly changing the subject. He had a lot to think about.

Jake pointed in the direction of a building they'd added a few years ago. They called it the Bachelor Pad since all the male cousins lived there.

"We've got room for you in the main house, of course, now that the boys, all except Casey, are out there, but I figured you'd want to be a little independent."

Toby nodded. "Why isn't Casey out there?"

"Aw, you know Janie. She considers Casey to be her miracle baby. She's not quite ready to turn him loose."

Pete and Janie had had the first of the babies, the twins, but she'd had a hard time. She'd hoped for a little girl the next time, but she never got pregnant. Then, when she'd given up on having another baby, she found herself pregnant just after the twins turned ten. Pete tried to save Casey from her coddling, but Janie was stubborn.

"Hey, Pete might be able to move the boy out there if you're going to live in the Pad. I'll suggest it to him. He's afraid the boy will be timid," Jake added with a laugh. "I don't really think he's got anything to worry about. The twins give Casey a hard time for the same reason."

Toby grinned. Life was normal at the Randalls.

"Wow," Toby suddenly exclaimed. "That will leave you with no kids in the house. Won't that seem strange?"

"Yep. When I started the matchmaking, I never envisioned it would be so successful." Toby and Jake shared a smile. Jake and his three brothers had lived for a number of years without any women. Jake had married Chloe, who divorced him and tried to take the ranch away from them. "Fear of Chloe" kept them from commitment until Jake realized they'd never have heirs to inherit the ranch unless something changed. So he hatched some matchmaking plots that really worked. "It seems sort of sad, though. I'll miss having little ones underfoot. 'Course, Elizabeth will live with us until the wedding."

"Uh, have they set a date?"

"Nope. I asked Chad about it and he said he wasn't in any hurry. He's hoping Elizabeth will come to her senses."

Toby frowned. "The moms aren't doing any manipulating, are they?"

Jake grinned again. "Naw. Not much."

"What do you mean not much?" Toby didn't want Elizabeth to be unhappy, but she'd made her choice. If she was going to marry the guy, they might as well get it over with and marry...and move.

"I guess you don't remember when Brett got engaged, do you?"

"To Anna?"

"Nope. Anna was here to help Janie deliver the twins, but Brett was in Cheyenne. When he got home and met Anna, he was already engaged to a senator's daughter. A real, uh...female Cleve."

"How awful. What did the moms do?"

"Nothing evil. They invited his fiancée to come to the ranch for a visit. And then let nature take its course. Within a couple of days, Brett realized Anna was the lady for him, thank God."

"They think if Cleve visits the ranch, Elizabeth will see that he doesn't fit in?"

"How could she help it? So, with you and Elizabeth coming home at the same time, we're feeling real lucky."

Toby offered up a smile, but it didn't match his father's grin. Real lucky. Oh, yeah. He didn't think that was what he'd call it.

ELIZABETH had to be up early the next morning for class, so she said goodbye to Cleve on the back porch at night.

"I wish you'd go for a drive with me, Elizabeth. It's not that late," Cleve pleaded.

"I can't, Cleve. I like to get to school early. Some of my babies are dropped off at seven-thirty because of the bus schedule. I don't like to leave them unsupervised."

"I don't know why you took the job. You'll just quit once we're married. You won't even finish the semester."

Elizabeth frowned. "What are you saying? I have no intention of quitting just because we get married."

"Of course you'll quit. I'll expect you to be my wife."

"What does that have to do with anything?" This topic hadn't come up in the two weeks they'd been engaged.

"You'll keep house, do volunteer work, have intimate dinners, things to promote my career." He smiled with satisfaction, obviously envisioning their future differently than her.

"Intimate dinners aren't exactly in style in Rawhide," she pointed out.

"Well, we won't be in Rawhide all that long. You can practice for when we move to Denver." Assuming she was in agreement, he put his arms around her and pulled her close.

Elizabeth shoved against his suit jacket. "Why would we move to Denver?"

"Because I don't intend to stay in a small pond forever. I'm made for bigger and better things." He leaned over to nuzzle her neck, and she jumped back, making it impossible to touch her.

"What's wrong?" he demanded, irritation in his voice. "I'm waiting, just like you asked, but surely I can touch you."

She couldn't argue that. He'd wanted her to sleep with him after their third date. She'd refused. He said he'd be patient. But his patience disappeared. Then he'd asked her to marry him and assumed he'd pushed the Go button.

Their engagement had almost ended in half an hour. When he finally understood that she intended to marry as a virgin, he'd reluctantly accepted her decision. But he pushed the limits every time.

Elizabeth held herself stiffly. "Cleve, you're making some assumptions that aren't true. I don't want to move to Denver. I want to stay here."

"Don't be silly, Elizabeth. I can't live on what I'll be making with this hick Bill Johnson."

"You don't like Bill?"

"Who cares if I like him? Don't tell me he's another Randall cousin. You've got enough of them already. And no more kissing the newest one."

Elizabeth knew he was referring to the kisses she'd given Toby when she'd first seen him. She didn't think that would happen again. Toby was too distant.

Too—too changed. But she wasn't ready to accept limitations on her behavior.

"Cleve, I think you'd better go. I've got some thinking to do."

"Okay. I'm going back to Laramie early tomorrow morning, but I'll call you." He managed to snatch a brief kiss, seemingly unaware that he'd upset her.

When he'd left, Elizabeth remained on the porch, enjoying the privacy. What had she done? In Laramie, Cleve had seemed sophisticated, well-mannered. He was handsome, smart, active on campus. When he'd proposed, she'd explained that she intended to go back to her home to teach school. He'd agreed.

But apparently his agreement was only temporary. He'd already made plans to move and assumed she'd accompany him.

With a sigh, she turned back to go inside. She'd end the engagement. He wasn't leaving her any choice.

A sound behind her had her spinning around. In the shadows, she recognized Toby.

"Where have you been?" she asked.

He stepped up on the porch, but he didn't show any enthusiasm about joining her.

"Out at the barn."

"Your horses all right?"

"Yeah, fine."

She couldn't think of anything else to say. They used to talk nonstop when they were younger. But as she'd noted earlier, Toby had changed. "What made you decide to drop out of rodeo and come home?"

"It wasn't because I was losing," he said, "like Caroline said."

She raised her eyebrows. "Caro was teasing. She brags about you all the time. She has tons of friends because they're hoping she'll introduce them to you."

His cheeks darkened, just barely visible. It was a charming part of Toby. He was unimpressed with his achievements.

She watched him shrug his shoulders instead of answer her original question. "Aren't you going to tell me?"

"Why should I? We don't share secrets anymore. You certainly haven't said why you're marrying that idiot! I thought you were supposed to get smarter in college, not take leave of your senses."

The abrupt attack stunned Elizabeth. "How dare you call me dumb! I have a right to my own choices! You don't even know Cleve." Why was she defending the man when she had no intention of marrying him? But it was only fair to tell him first, not Toby. Especially not Toby when he was insulting her intelligence.

"I know him more than I ever want to. He's an accountant and he thinks he's superior to us?" Toby's scorn was evident.

"Uncle Brett is an accountant. It's a perfectly good job."

"Uncle Brett is a rancher. He does accounting for the family. That's different."

"So Bill Johnson is—"

"I'm not arguing this," he muttered, walking past her to reach the back door.

"What's the matter? Afraid you'll lose?"

Her taunting had the desired effect. He pulled to a halt and turned around to stare at her. "You've certainly changed, Elizabeth. I don't remember you being so difficult."

"I'm surprised you remember me at all, it's been so long since I've seen you. I used to— I guess you've been more interested in…other things than your family."

He stared at her, his breathing rough. Then, much to her disappointment, he muttered, "I guess I have."

Before she could say anything else, he disappeared into the house.

A single tear escaped her eye to flow silently down her cheek. She remembered a picture in a cowboy magazine of Toby surrounded by beautiful women putting their hands all over him. She'd hated that picture, told herself it didn't represent Toby's real life. He probably didn't know any of those women. They were just models.

Now she wasn't so sure.

Maybe he was biding his time before he brought one of them home as his wife. Or maybe he intended to cut a wide swath through Rawhide and the surrounding ranches with all the single women. She immediately started making a mental list of women he would discover.

As she went back in the house to go to bed, she didn't give her engagement to Cleve a thought. What Toby was going to do was much more important.

THOUGH ALL the male cousins had moved to the Pad, they always ate their meals with the family. Toby figured he wouldn't have to worry about seeing Elizabeth at breakfast. After all, schools didn't start until eight in the morning. He'd have been in the saddle for at least an hour by then.

He came into the kitchen the next morning at six-thirty, the normal time, and discovered Elizabeth helping Mildred to set the table.

Mildred sang out, "Morning! So good to see you here, Toby!"

"Hey, now," Russ called, "no giving Toby more food than us."

Mildred grinned. "Might be a good idea. I think you're puttin' on weight, Russ."

Though he was tall and lean, Russ pretended to be wounded by Mildred's teasing. With laughter, the guys sat down. Their fathers would come a few minutes later. Red called it the second wave.

It was the younger Randalls' job to have the horses saddled when their fathers finished eating. Jake called it the privilege of rank.

"What are you doing up?" Toby asked Elizabeth abruptly.

"I leave for school at seven," she replied, not looking at him.

"Do Drew and Casey ride with you?" He noticed the two boys weren't there for breakfast.

"No, they like to wait until seven-thirty before they go. Drew takes a truck." She didn't know why it mattered. Drew was a senior, certainly old enough to drive.

Red nudged Toby toward the table. "I'm serving your eggs, boy. Sit down and eat."

Toby did so, but his mind seemed to be on Elizabeth since he continued talking to her. "In winter it's going to be dark at seven. I don't think you should drive alone when it's dark."

Everyone stopped what they were doing and stared at Toby.

Jim, her brother, spoke up before Elizabeth did. She was too stunned by Toby's words.

"It's only ten or twelve miles, Toby. Elizabeth is a good driver."

"But—" Toby began, but Elizabeth found her voice.

"It doesn't matter what you think, Toby. If my father doesn't have a problem with my behavior, I think you can stop worrying."

"What does Cleve think about it?" he asked.

Since last night he'd called Cleve dumb, she didn't understand why Toby would care about his attitude. And she wasn't about to tell him that Cleve didn't want her to teach at all. Maybe both men were more macho than she'd thought.

"Didn't your mother work in the winter? I believe she's gone out in the dark to work on dangerous animals. And Anna goes out to deliver babies at all hours of the day and night."

"Yeah, but Uncle Brett goes with her after dark," Rich pointed out.

Elizabeth glared at her helpful cousin.

Red interrupted. "Eat your breakfasts. I hear boots on the stairway."

"And mind your own business," Elizabeth muttered under her breath to Toby. She wasn't about to let him tell her what to do when he wouldn't even speak to her nicely.

The rest of the meal was a fast scramble as the guys gobbled down their breakfasts and carried their plates to the sink just as the older generation entered the room.

Elizabeth was glad Toby left the kitchen as the others took their places, only exchanging a few words with his father. He wouldn't discuss her going to school alone with his father, she was sure.

When Toby left the house, Jake sighed with a big grin on his face. "Man, it's good to have him back home." He looked at B.J. "Isn't it, sweetheart?"

"Of course."

"What did he say last night when you talked to him?" Pete asked.

"How'd you know I talked to him?" Jake demanded.

Pete shrugged his shoulders. "'Cause I know you. The boy's the biggest success in rodeo in years. I think he was on track for another Cowboy of the Year. Do you think he's running away from a broken heart?"

Elizabeth kept her head down, but she listened intently.

"Didn't mention a woman. I think something's wrong," he admitted, patting B.J.'s hand as she let a slight gasp escape. "He seems okay with his decision, but I told him we'd understand if he changes his mind. We wouldn't be any worse off if he leaves again."

They all nodded, as if in agreement, but Elizabeth had to hold back. She wanted to protest, to tell Jake he couldn't let Toby leave again. But it wasn't her business. And why did she think he shouldn't go away again? She didn't want to answer that question.

Red brought her out of her thoughts. "I fixed you lunch, Elizabeth. Don't forget it."

"I won't, Red, but I'm going to gain weight if you don't put less in it."

"You need some meat on your bones, little girl. Some of those students are bigger than you."

Elizabeth choked on her orange juice. "Red, I teach kindergarten!"

"But they still have big kids at the school. Those seniors can be difficult."

Red's words ended just as Drew, a senior, entered. Red immediately dished up food for him.

"Maybe you shouldn't feed Drew so much, Red. After all, he's one of those dreaded seniors," Elizabeth said, grinning.

"Hey, what did I do?" Drew asked, watching Red fill his plate.

"Nothing, dear," Megan reassured him. "Red was concerned that some of you are bigger than Elizabeth."

Drew snorted in disgust. "You bet we are. We'd all be shrimps if we weren't."

Everyone smiled, but Jake added, "Say, Pete, I wondered if you wanted to let Casey move out with the guys now that Toby's back. He'd keep an eye on him."

Janie protested at once, but Pete threw him a grateful look. "That's a good idea."

Elizabeth thought they were mistaken about Toby watching out for Casey. The old Toby would have, but the new one didn't seem to care that much…in her opinion. But she didn't say anything because she knew how badly Casey wanted to be counted as a grown-up.

She'd decided for several reasons she'd better be on her way when the phone rang.

Everyone stared at it. There weren't many calls in the morning except for emergencies. B.J. grabbed it. She and Anna frequently received those kinds of calls.

With a puzzled look, she said, "Yes, just a minute." Then she turned to Elizabeth. "It's for you."

Elizabeth frowned too as she took the phone.

"Elizabeth, this is Bill Johnson. Is your fiancé there?"

"No, he's leaving this morning for Laramie. Did you try the motel?"

"Yep. I guess he's gone."

"Is there a problem?"

"Well, maybe. Can I speak to you after class today?"

"Of course. I'll come by as soon as I've finished."

"Good. I'll—I'll see you then."

Chapter Three

Elizabeth wondered what Bill Johnson had to say to her, but she didn't have a lot of time to think about it. Her morning class consisted of seventeen five-year-olds. If she took her gaze off them even for a minute, they got into trouble. But she loved their energy.

When she did think of something else, her mind seemed naturally to flow to Toby, wondering about his first day working on the ranch. And why he'd come back. Not many people turned down fame and fortune.

She also wondered why he'd changed so much. She missed the Toby of her childhood, her teenage years...until she'd reached the age of sixteen. When she'd cried the last time he'd come home from college, her mother had explained that Toby probably had a girlfriend at school and his mind was on her.

"Miss Randall? Isn't it time to go?" Davey, one of her brightest pupils, asked, staring at the big clock on the wall.

"Oh, yes, it is. Okay, let's line up." Times had

changed. The kindergarteners were never released until someone came for them. A number of them rode a small bus to a childcare center nearby. The rest of them were claimed by their parents. Once Elizabeth had delivered each child to a guardian, she had an hour to eat lunch and prepare for the afternoon group. It was smaller because the morning was the preferred time. Most of the children scheduled for the afternoon were the oldest and soon to turn six.

Elizabeth headed for the teachers' lounge and the refrigerator where she'd left her lunch. Then she settled at the round table. The lounge was filled with cast-off furniture, but it was actually a pleasant room. Just as she sat down, one of the first-grade teachers, also a native of the area, joined her.

"I heard Toby's back home! Is he going to stay a while?" Abby Gaylord asked, her eyes sparkling.

"News travels fast around here. He just came back last night."

"I know, but he's famous. And rich. And the last I heard he was still single."

"That's the last I've heard, too," Elizabeth admitted reluctantly. "But that doesn't mean he doesn't have a lady. He's not acting like himself."

"Ooh! I bet he has a broken heart! I'll be glad to console him." Abby's gaze was intent on Elizabeth.

"Did you want me to tell him that?"

"No! Don't be silly. He wouldn't look at me. Not with you hanging around," Abby said with a wry smile.

Elizabeth concentrated on her sandwich. "He's my cousin."

"Honey, there's no blood kinship. Everyone knows that."

Elizabeth's heartbeat sped up. She'd never admitted to anyone in the family that she'd finally figured that out when she was sixteen. Toby was considered a Randall in every way. For almost a year Elizabeth had held that information close to her heart. Then Toby's behavior had told her it didn't matter.

"Do you think he'll come to the big Halloween party?"

Elizabeth stared at the other woman. "That's two months away."

"I know, but we could get him to sign autographs for a dollar and make a lot of money for the teachers' fund."

"I can ask him. I'm not sure he'll be here by then, but I'll check with him."

"Thanks, Elizabeth. Or he could have a kissing booth for five dollars a kiss. Then we'd really make a killing."

Elizabeth ended that idea. "No. Toby wouldn't like that." *She* wouldn't like it, whether he did or not.

"Okay. Just a thought. But ask him about doing autographs. That would be great. Oh, I've got a better idea. We could have a raffle and the winner gets a date with Toby. Yeah, he could do that and the autographs. It wouldn't kill him to spend one evening with a local lady, Elizabeth. Please ask him."

Elizabeth didn't like that idea either. But it was more reasonable than him kissing a hundred women. With a sigh she promised she would.

"Is he still as good-looking as ever?"

Elizabeth was fast developing a headache. "Yes."

"Come on. Aren't you going to give me some details?" Abby asked, practically salivating as she waited.

"No. Abby, you've known him all your life. He looks the same."

Abby sighed and lapsed into silence, staring into space.

Elizabeth knew what her friend was seeing in her mind. A tall man, muscular, but rangy, with a singular grace, light brown, almost golden eyes, dark hair, strong features…and a beautiful smile that varied between cocky and sympathetic. The desire to be the center of his universe, to have that smile all to herself, had long been her secret wish.

"How's your class today?" Elizabeth asked, desperate to change the subject.

For the remaining minutes before Abby's next class, they discussed work. But when Abby left, the next arrivals wanted to talk about Toby, too. One of the teachers had taught him years ago and always thought of him as that same little boy. At least that was a better image than Toby in a kissing booth.

When she was ready to go home, she checked her calendar for the next day and saw the note she'd written about Bill Johnson. Otherwise, she would've gone straight home, her mind focused on Toby.

She drove the short distance to Bill Johnson's office on the main street of Rawhide. He never used a receptionist or secretary, so she knocked on the open door of his office and he looked up from his desk.

"Oh, Elizabeth, thanks for coming by," he said, rising to shake her hand. "Sit down, please."

Elizabeth did so and waited for him to speak.

"Uh, Mr. O'Banyon came in yesterday afternoon, you know. We'd corresponded, of course, and he has excellent skills." He paused and stared at her.

"And?"

"Elizabeth, I've been friends with your family for a long time. I'd do anything I could to help them, but—" He broke off again.

Elizabeth smiled. She realized his dilemma. "You don't think you can work with Cleve?"

Relief filled his face. "Not just me. My customers—they wouldn't come back. He, uh, sneers at the way people dress here. He actually made fun of Mr. Holliwell when he came in while O'Banyon was here."

"Oh, I'm so sorry, Bill. But deciding not to hire him won't affect your friendship with my family. Have you spoken with Cleve?"

Bill nodded. "Yeah. He didn't take it well."

"I'm not surprised. He thinks he would be an asset to any company."

Bill looked at her sharply, and she knew she hadn't hidden her disgust well.

"Uh, well, I appreciate your understanding."

"Do you still need help?"

He stared at her warily. "Yeah, but—"

"I was going to suggest you talk to my cousin, Russ."

"Russ is looking for a job as an accountant?" Bill asked, surprise in his voice.

"Not exactly. But he majored in accounting, and I think he'd like to work in town part-time."

"I had no idea. That's a great idea! I'll call him this evening."

"Mmm, could you wait until next week?"

"Why?"

"I need to talk to my family after I've talked to Cleve, and I won't be able to manage all that until the weekend." She really felt she should tell Cleve first that she'd changed her mind.

"Okay, as long as you don't think anyone else would snap him up. He'll be perfect."

"How do you know? He might not know enough accounting," she pointed out.

"Randalls breed true, Elizabeth. There hasn't been a bad one yet." His grin was wide and warm.

Elizabeth smiled back. But she realized she might've broken that chain if she'd married Cleve and had his children. Why hadn't she realized that earlier? She stood. "Thanks for your cooperation, Bill. We'll have everything settled very soon."

"I appreciate that, Elizabeth."

DARK WAS STARTING to come earlier, and Toby was glad. His first day back in the saddle took a lot of stamina. He was strong and skilled, but he was tired.

"Good job today, Toby," his Uncle Pete said, pulling up beside him. "I figure we got a lot more done today with your roping skills."

"You're no slouch yourself, Uncle Pete." His uncle was the only one of the Randalls before Toby who had rodeo experience.

"I wanted to tell you I appreciate you not encouraging the boys to head out for the rodeo, too. Rich has mentioned going several times, but Russ always reminds him about what you said."

Toby grinned. "I didn't want them making that their life. It's too hard, and it can lead them down the wrong path."

"True. So why did you stay so long?"

Toby stiffened. He hadn't been prepared for that question. "I wanted to earn enough to pay for my own place."

"Oh. Have you talked to your dad about land around here? I'm sure he'd be glad to help you."

"I'm in no hurry." He'd already decided if Elizabeth and Cleve settled down in Rawhide, he wouldn't be doing the same. He told himself she'd be married then, but it didn't seem to affect his hormones.

"Your dad—"

Toby interrupted. "I'd appreciate your not mentioning this to Dad just yet. I want to enjoy being home with the family for a while.''

''Sure thing, boy. Jake loves having you home.''

''I love being here,'' Toby returned as they reached the barn, and he caught sight of Elizabeth's car. She was home. He started trying to stifle the desire that rose up in him. Damn, he only had to know she was there, without even seeing her, to start yearning for her.

After taking care of his horse, he headed for the Pad with Russ and Rich, telling his father he was going to clean up.

''Okay. Red will ring when dinner is ready,'' Jake assured him.

With a wave, he walked with the cousins.

''Hey, we didn't have a chance to ask last night,'' Rich began. ''You haven't told us about any of the women.''

''What women?'' Toby asked, his mind on Elizabeth.

''The women that chase all the rodeo guys,'' Russ explained.

Toby shrugged his shoulders. ''There's not much to tell.''

''Come on, Toby!'' Rich protested. ''Don't tell me you've lived like a monk all these years.''

Toby knew his cousins would be shocked if he told them how seldom he'd indulged in feminine company...and how dissatisfying those few encounters had been. "Guys, those women are like the ones who hang out in a bar hoping to pick up a man for the night."

Russ frowned, considering his words. Rich grinned. "Some of them aren't so bad."

"Yeah, but do you want one of them as mother to your children?"

Rich frowned then. "Of course not! But one night doesn't make a marriage."

"Depends on whether or not you're lucky, friend," Toby pointed out. "If you play with fire, you can get burned."

"You sound like Dad," Rich protested.

"Uncle Pete is a pretty smart man. Besides, there are some great ladies around here."

"I haven't seen you courting anyone," Rich said. "I think you're just saving all those models for yourself."

"Models aren't interested in settling down."

"That's the good part," Rich explained. "Neither am I."

Toby chuckled and shook his head. He'd try to knock some sense into Rich's head later.

"Toby?"

The feminine voice brought him to an immediate stop. He'd recognize Elizabeth's tones anywhere. Turning slowly, he said, "Yes, Elizabeth?"

"Could I talk to you a minute?"

"How about after I clean up?"

"It won't take long."

She had an anxious look on her face, and he couldn't reject her. So much for being strong. "Yeah, sure. I'll be in in a minute, guys."

There was a bench on the porch of the Pad. Without any urging on his part, Elizabeth sat down. She was still wearing the blue-jean jumper and pale blue blouse she'd worn to school that morning. Her blue eyes looked huge.

He put a booted foot on the bench but didn't sit down. He didn't trust himself to get that close. "What is it?"

"Uh, I'm supposed to— You're really staying?"

Toby drew a deep breath, taking in her sweet scent. His hands tingled with the desire to touch her, to press her against him and tell her he'd stay forever if she wanted him to.

But ever since he'd realized, the summer she turned sixteen, that his feelings for Elizabeth weren't cousinly, he'd fought them. Elizabeth was his cousin, even if not by blood. His father would be horrified if he admitted the truth. And the one thing in life he wanted to accomplish was to make Jake proud. Not shame him.

"Why do you want to know?"

She gave him a funny stare. "But you said—"

"Okay, I'm staying, at least for a while. What do you want?"

"Abby—you remember Abby Gaylord, don't you?"

"Yeah." He was getting impatient. It was draining

to resist Elizabeth and he was already tired. Who cared about Abby Gaylord?

"She wanted me to ask you— We have the Halloween festival for the area, remember, at school?"

"Yeah!" he snapped, wondering where this was going.

Elizabeth stood and crossed her arms over her chest. "You don't have to growl at me. I'm asking you because Abby asked me to."

"What? What are you asking me?" he persisted, trying to sound like a reasonable man when she was driving him crazy.

"She wondered if you'd sign autographs for a dollar and give the money to the teachers' fund."

The teachers' fund? That hadn't been what Toby expected. "What's the teachers' fund?"

"We try to make money each year and give a scholarship to a deserving student. And the rest is used to buy cards, or goodbye gifts, or flowers for funerals, things like that."

"Are you a member?"

"Of course I am. Will you do it?"

"I don't usually charge for autographs."

"But it's for a good cause."

With a sigh, he said, "Yeah, okay." As he took his foot down and turned to go in the Pad, she stopped him again.

"Wait!"

"What? I agreed."

"I know but—but Abby had another idea."

He thought she seemed even more reluctant about the second idea than she had the first. Warily, he asked what the second idea was.

"She wants to hold a raffle."

Toby frowned. "What does that have to do with me?"

"Um...you're the prize." She stared at him, wariness in her eyes.

He exploded. "What? I'm not a prize. What are you talking about?"

The door opened and Rich and Russ, fresh from their showers, stepped out on the porch. "Wow, Elizabeth, you must be in big trouble if it takes you this long to convince Toby to get you out of hot water," Russ said with a grin.

"I'm not in trouble!"

"You sure? You're still engaged to that, uh, to Cleve, aren't you?" Rich pointed out.

"That has nothing to do with what we're talking about."

"Okay," Rich continued. "But I was going to offer to help if that was what you wanted."

"Go away!" Elizabeth shouted at them.

"Why don't you ask one of them to do the raffle," Toby suggested. "I don't want to hog all the fun."

"What raffle?" Russ asked.

"It's for the Halloween festival," Elizabeth explained.

But Toby knew she was in a difficult position. She didn't want to hurt her cousins' feelings by telling them they weren't important enough for the raffle. She shifted her gaze to Toby, as if asking him to get her out of the bind, but he just smiled and waited.

A sudden glint in her eye alarmed him, however. She no longer was looking helpless. "You're right, Toby. You should all get the same treatment. We'll have a bachelor auction, and you can all participate."

"Wait a minute. What do you mean a bachelor auction?" Russ questioned. "I'm not ready to get married."

"Don't be silly," Elizabeth said with a smile directed at Toby. "You'll each provide a picnic dinner and whoever pays for your picnic will share it with you. It's the reversal of what women used to do to raise money."

"You won't have anyone volunteer for that," Toby assured her.

"But you're only committed for a picnic dinner and we'll raise a lot of money. You'll do it, guys, won't you?" Elizabeth asked sweetly, smiling at them. "It's for a good cause."

"Aw, I guess," Russ agreed, "since it's for a good cause. If Red will agree to fix the dinners for us."

"I'm sure he will," Elizabeth said with a smile. "You will, too, won't you, Rich?"

The second twin nodded, a rueful smile on his lips.

"And Toby? Unless, of course, you feel you're too important to participate."

He was ready to wring her neck. She'd trapped him

into agreeing with her plan or look like a jerk to his cousins.

"Well, Toby?" she prodded.

"Yeah, sure. Now can I go get cleaned up before dinner is ready?"

"Yes, thank you. I'll tell Abby you're volunteering." She smiled before turning and hurrying to the main house.

"You know, this kind of sounds like fun," Russ said, grinning. "It saves us the trouble of finding a date, but it guarantees we won't end the evening alone."

"Maybe," Rich agreed. "It depends on who bids for my picnic basket."

"Hey, if they think Red made the food, they'll all bid for it."

"You idiot!" Rich said with a hoot of laughter. "Women don't care about the food. They just want to jump your bones."

"Even better," Russ said. "Right, Toby?"

Toby still had his gaze fixed on the back door of the house where Elizabeth had disappeared.

"Uh, yeah. Right." He'd even be okay with the idea if Elizabeth were one of the ladies bidding. He'd pray for luck. But she wouldn't be. She was engaged. Maybe she'd even be married by then.

"I'm going in to shower. Save me some food."

Chapter Four

Elizabeth had put in a call for Cleve, leaving a message on his answering machine. Unfortunately, his return call came in the middle of dinner.

Elizabeth took the phone from Anna, who had answered, with her entire family looking on.

"Uh, Cleve, we're in the middle of dinner. Will you be home later?"

"No, I won't, Elizabeth. Why are you calling?"

"I spoke with Bill Johnson today," she whispered, turning her back on the family.

"Don't tell me you're worried about us making enough money. I'll take care of you, babe. Or we can get a loan from your dad."

"Cleve, we have to talk. When can you come up?" She had no doubt about her decision now. The man thought they could live off her parents? Had he asked her to marry him because of her father's money? Disgust filled her.

"I'll be up on the weekend. I can't get away before then."

"Fine," she snapped and hung up the phone. She knew it was rude, but she couldn't talk to him any longer without dropping her bombshell by phone. And that would really be rude.

When she turned back to face the family, they were all staring at her.

Then Megan politely asked, "How is Cleve?"

"Fine," she said calmly just before the phone rang again. She leaped to her feet and answered. "Hello."

"Why did you hang up on me? I won't tolerate that kind of behavior, Elizabeth."

She sighed. Just what she wanted, more conversation with Cleve. "I can't talk now, Cleve. I'll see you Friday."

"Okay, fine, but I don't see any point to my coming if you're going to be rude."

"Goodbye," she said firmly, then hung up the phone again.

This time when she turned around, everyone averted their eyes, but Elizabeth knew they were all dying to know what was going on. "Cleve forgot something he needed to tell me."

"Didn't sound like a friendly goodbye," Chad, her father, commented.

She knew her father didn't like Cleve. Instead of things getting better as they got to know each other, they only seemed to get worse.

"Chad," Megan reprimanded with a frown, "I don't think that's any of your business. I'm sure Elizabeth would tell us if there's a problem."

Elizabeth smiled politely and said nothing, keeping her gaze averted.

Before the silence grew too strained, Toby said, "Elizabeth has big plans for the Halloween party this year."

That topic got the family's attention, for which Elizabeth was grateful. The twins spoke up at once.

"Yeah, we're going to be auctioned off," Russ said.

"Oh, really?" Mildred exclaimed. "Remember when we auctioned off lunches for the church roof fund? Is it the same kind of deal?"

"Uh, yes. The men will bring a picnic dinner and the single ladies can bid on them. To raise money for the teachers' fund. And Toby, Russ and Rich have agreed to participate." Elizabeth flashed a grateful smile at the three.

"Hey! What about us?" Josh demanded. "Jim and I should get to sign up for it, too. After all, we're college men."

"But you'll be away at college, Josh," Elizabeth pointed out.

"We could come home for the weekend."

Elizabeth looked at her mother, Megan, for guidance.

"It would help raise more money," she pointed out.

"But you probably should limit it to twenty-one or older," Chad suggested, "for legality's sake."

Elizabeth didn't know what to say. "I'd better consult with Abby Gaylord before I make any decisions. She's in charge of our projects."

"Abby? I should've known she was involved in this," Russ said in disgruntled tones.

"Why do you say that?" Janie, his mother, asked. "Abby is a very nice young lady."

"Yeah. Too nice," Rich contributed. "She was always getting us in trouble at school."

"I didn't hear about you getting in trouble at school," Janie pointed out, staring at her sons with speculation in her eyes. "Do you want to explain?"

"Uh, no, Mom. Rich was just kidding. Right, Rich?" Russ added. Then he looked at Red. "Dinner is really great, Red. Did you put something different in the meat loaf tonight?"

Several of the adults, including Toby, smiled. Elizabeth, too, realized Russ was trying to redirect the conversation.

"Is Cleve going to participate in the auction?" Chad asked. He stared at Elizabeth.

"Um, I doubt it. He doesn't know anyone around here except for the family," Elizabeth said, again avoiding her father's gaze.

"It would give him a chance to make new friends," Jake offered.

His wife protested. "Elizabeth and Cleve might be married by then. Honey," she added, looking at Elizabeth, "have you and Cleve looked for a place to live?"

"No, not really. I don't think we'll be married before Halloween, so there's plenty of time."

Elizabeth changed the subject, telling about people asking about Toby coming home, centering the attention on him instead of her.

When dinner was over, Toby volunteered to be in charge of cleanup. Red and Mildred were seldom allowed to do the cleaning. After all, Red was seventy-four and Mildred seventy-one. It was enough for them to do all the cooking.

In spite of the younger guys' complaints, everyone else began to leave the room. Then B.J. noticed her husband and his brothers were remaining at the table.

"Aren't you coming, Jake?" she asked.

"Aw, honey, we want to watch the boys, see if they take care of everything. It does our old bodies good to see them working more."

The ladies all left the room, chuckling.

Once the door had closed, Toby looked at his stepfather. "You don't trust us to clean up?"

"Hell, boy, I'd trust you with anything. But Chad has something he wants to ask you and, well, I'm supporting him."

"Us, too," Brett added. Pete nodded.

Toby frowned, worried about what they were going to ask. He was already trapped into the bachelor auction. He didn't need any more traps.

Chad cleared his throat. "Boy, you remember how you took care of Caro and Lizzie when you were younger? How those two little girls followed you around, willing to do anything you told them to do?''

Toby nodded, but he was getting a sinking feeling in his stomach. ''Yeah, but that was a long time ago.''

''I know it was, but—but I'm desperate.''

''What is it, Dad?'' Jim asked. ''Drew and I could help.''

''I appreciate the offer, Jim, but I don't think you and Drew could convince Elizabeth.''

''Uh-oh,'' Jim muttered. ''You're right.''

Toby looked at Jim sharply, but he didn't ask what they were talking about. He was pretty sure he knew.

''Toby,'' Chad said, ''I want you to talk to Elizabeth about marrying this Cleve. She needs to take some time to think about what she's doing. The man is a stiff. He doesn't fit in around here and never will. I think he's marrying her because he thinks we'll give him money.''

''Well, he could be right,'' Brett said, grinning. ''You'd give him money to get lost.''

''Yeah, if I thought it would work. But Toby could talk her out of it. Couldn't you, Toby?''

''I don't think—that is, Elizabeth is a woman now. As hardheaded as any of them, Uncle Chad. I don't think she'd listen to me.''

''But would you just try?''

While Toby was trying to figure out how he could turn down Chad's plea, Pete said, ''Makes me glad I only had boys, even if they are ornery.''

''I think maybe we're not giving Cleve a chance,''

Toby said carefully. "After all, he's the first one to want to marry into the family. Maybe we're all over-reacting."

Jake shook his head. "It's not that, son. We'd love to have more babies in the family. But his babies? Ugh! I think you should help Chad out here."

"Dad—" Toby began, but he couldn't resist his stepfather's request. With a sigh he replied, "Okay, fine, I'll try to talk to Elizabeth, but I don't think it will do any good."

As if afraid Toby might change his mind suddenly, the older generation fled the kitchen, leaving Toby with his cousins.

"Sucker," Toby's brother said. "You know you can't talk a woman *out* of love. Into love, maybe, but not out of love."

"What could I do? You saw their faces. I couldn't say no."

"Well, I think—" Russ began when the kitchen door opened.

Elizabeth walked into the kitchen, her eyes fastened on Toby. "Dad said you wanted to talk to me, Toby. What about?"

Damn it, they hadn't even left the timing up to him. "Uh, yeah, but I need to finish the cleaning up." At least he could stall until he'd gathered his thoughts.

"Don't worry about that, Tobe," Rich sang out, a grin on his face. "We'll take care of it. Don't keep Elizabeth waiting."

Toby turned away from Elizabeth, so she couldn't

see his expression. "Thanks, Rich, I'll be sure to pay you back." His expressions conveyed his meaning to his cousin.

Rich stepped closer to his brother. "No need," he said.

"Oh, yeah, Rich. You know I don't like to *owe* anyone." Toby gave him a fierce smile that wiped the smile off his cousin's face.

"Elizabeth, why don't we walk to the barn. I need to see if Cocoa is doing okay after all our hard work today."

She crossed the kitchen to the back door and Toby followed, frantically trying to think how to approach such a delicate subject.

The night air was cooling these days, ready for the move into fall. Toby took a deep breath. "You warm enough?" he asked.

"Yes, I'm fine. What's going on? It seemed to me that the others know what the discussion is about. What do we need to talk about? Are you trying to get out of the bachelor auction?"

"No, of course not. I gave my word."

"Well, then, what?"

Toby stopped by the corral and propped one of his feet on the lowest rail, hanging his arms over the top one and called to Cocoa. "Do you remember when you named him?"

Distracted, Elizabeth reached out to pet the horse when he came near. "Of course. I was thrilled. Is he still your favorite?"

"Yeah. He's the best ever." Toby stroked the horse also, until his fingers accidently touched Elizabeth's. He jerked his hands back. But he figured he'd distracted her from their topic of conversation.

"So what did Dad ask you to talk about? Cleve?"

So much for distraction. It didn't seem to be his specialty. "How did you know?"

"Because Dad has let me know how disappointed he is about my choice," Elizabeth stated calmly.

"And that doesn't bother you?"

"Of course it does! But I also don't think he's given Cleve a fair shake. And that's not like Daddy."

"Maybe Uncle Chad knows more about Cleve than you do. Can't you trust your father's instincts?"

"Do you trust *your* father's instincts?" she asked, turning the tables on him.

"Of course I do!"

"Then why did you hit the rodeo trail? You knew he didn't want you to, didn't you? We certainly all realized it. He and B.J. were depressed for months after you left."

"That's not fair, Elizabeth. Dad and Mom may not've wanted me to go, but there was nothing dangerous about it."

Elizabeth laughed, but the sound didn't have any joy in it. "You think rodeoing isn't dangerous? I beg to differ. What about that man who died early this year because he landed on his head and had a concussion? Do you think his family would say there was nothing dangerous about rodeoing?"

"He was a beginner. Didn't know what he was doing."

"You were a beginner, too."

Toby sighed. He'd known this would be a disaster. "I was experienced. We'd done a lot of rodeoing ever since I was a kid. And we're not here to discuss the rodeo as a career choice. We're here to discuss your choice for a husband. Wasn't there anyone better?"

"Oh, I see, your theory is I just reached out and blindly selected the first man in sight, and it happened to be an intelligent, handsome man. Poor me."

"Your description is inaccurate. I'd say you grabbed a man who is arrogant, insensitive and stupid."

"Cleve made straight *A*s and *B*s," she protested hotly!

"I made straight *A*s, period." He glared at her.

"Well, everyone can't be perfect like Toby Randall!"

Toby turned his back to her. The temptation to grab her and kiss any thoughts of Cleve out of her head was too tempting. "I told your dad this wouldn't work."

"What wouldn't work?"

"He thought since you used to follow me around, you'd listen to my opinion on your choice."

"I followed you around when I was a child. And if I remember correctly, I stopped following you around because you made it plain you wanted me to go away so you could neck with your girlfriend!"

Toby couldn't hold back a rueful chuckle. "Well,

you and Caro did kind of hamper my love life for a while.''

Elizabeth crossed her arms over her chest and sniffed the night air in disgust. "I can assure you I won't do so again. But I have the right to ask the same promise from you."

"Honey, we're all only thinking of you. If there's one change in you I've definitely noticed, it's your stubbornness. But life with Cleve may take all your independence away. Because he's definitely that kind of man."

"And you're not?" she asked. "What do you call what you're doing now?"

"I'm asking you to think about what you're doing. To think about what you'll do when the man wants to move away. And you know he will. He's not going to be happy here. He won't be able to work with Bill Johnson. Then what are you going to do?"

She huffed and turned to head for the house. He grabbed her arm without thinking, then quickly released it. Touching her wasn't safe.

"Elizabeth?"

She spun around to stare at him. "Did it ever occur to you that I might figure out my own problems? That I'm not that little girl anymore? If I were, how would I have managed since you disappeared from my life? I've only seen you about half a day at Christmas each year since I was sixteen."

"I know I haven't been—I had my reasons for not hanging around the ranch. I couldn't make the money

I've made if I rodeoed only half the time. I had to dedicate myself to rodeo to do well."

"Right. And the perfect Toby Randall couldn't do anything only halfway. But don't expect me to hang around waiting to follow in your footsteps again. I make my own decisions now, and you can tell my father the same thing. I don't need a man telling me what to do."

Again she headed for the house, and this time he didn't try to stop her. It had been a disaster, just as he'd foreseen.

ELIZABETH STOMPED back to the house, pausing only once on the way to her bedroom. She stuck her head into the den where the parents were watching a movie. "Mom?" she called softly.

Her mother came to the door. "Yes?"

"I need to talk to you. Can you come by my room before you go to bed?"

Megan studied her face. "I'll come now," she said, stepping into the hallway and closing the door behind her.

"I don't want you to miss your movie," Elizabeth protested.

Megan took her hand and headed for the stairs.

Once they were in Elizabeth's bedroom, with the door closed, Megan asked, "What's wrong?"

"Dad asked Toby to talk to me about Cleve."

"He didn't!" She stared at her daughter. "I guess he did. But darling, you know it's because he loves you."

"I know, Mom, but it's a little embarrassing."

"Better to be embarrassed than to ruin your life," Megan said quietly.

"Oh, Mom, not you, too?"

Megan grinned. "Yeah, me, too. I haven't said anything because I think you'll figure it out soon, unless…well, unless you've gotten too involved with him? You're not pregnant, are you?"

"Mom!" Elizabeth protested. "Absolutely not!"

"Thank goodness."

"Look, I just need some time. Will you please trust me to do the right thing?"

"You mean you're going to—"

"I'm going to do the right thing for me. I'm asking you to trust me."

"Of course I trust you, darling. Did Toby's talk help you decide—"

"No! Mr. Arrogance himself called the kettle black, but I couldn't tell much difference between the two of them."

"Oh. Then how did you—"

"Mom, I can't discuss anything with you. I haven't talked to Clevè yet. Don't you think I should discuss everything with him first?"

"I guess so. But if I could just hint to your father, I could be sure of him staying out of your business." Megan stared at Elizabeth, hope in her gaze.

"Mom! Oh, okay, tell Daddy everything will be settled this weekend. But nothing else. Promise?"

"Of course, dear. And I'm so pleased." Megan

kissed her daughter good-night and slipped from the room.

Elizabeth felt she'd gone a ten-rounder with all her problems this evening. With a sigh, she prepared for bed, hoping tomorrow would be a better day.

MEGAN RETURNED to the den less unobtrusively than she'd left.

"What did she want?" Chad immediately asked. "Did he convince her?"

"She didn't say that. She complained about you not trusting her," Megan told him.

B.J. immediately turned off the television. "Did Toby make her mad?"

"She didn't say that either, but that would be my guess," Megan said, a grin on her face.

"Hell! Why would Toby make her mad?" Jake wanted to know. "He was only trying to help her."

Anna shook her head slowly, a big smile on her face. "All these years living with you, B.J., and he still doesn't understand women." All four women laughed.

"What's so funny?" Chad demanded. "My daughter is still engaged to that idiot."

"Your daughter sent you a message," Megan said. "Trust her and everything will be taken care of in a few days."

"She's going to elope?" Chad demanded, leaping to his feet, his fists clenched.

Chapter Five

Toby expected some fallout the next morning from Chad over his discussion with Elizabeth. Instead, his uncle patted him on the shoulder and thanked him for trying. Then he asked everyone to keep an eye on his only daughter.

"An eye out for what?" Rich asked as he swung into the saddle.

Chad looked at his brothers, then shrugged. "I think she may be planning on eloping."

Several of her cousins protested his suggestion.

Toby cleared his throat. "What makes you think that, Uncle Chad? I know I upset her, but—" He couldn't go on. He wanted Elizabeth married so he could come home, but he didn't want her unhappy. And she would be if she married that jerk.

"She wants me to trust her. Says everything will be settled this weekend!" Chad growled. "What else could she mean?"

"Maybe," Russ said hopefully, "she intends to dump him."

"If she were going to do that, why wait?" Chad asked. "She could pick up the phone and do it in five minutes. She's waiting because he won't be back here until the weekend, and it's hard to elope without a groom."

Toby couldn't argue with Chad's logic. He'd like to. He'd like to think Elizabeth wouldn't do that, but her dad was right. In this age of communication, it wouldn't take long to tell someone to get lost.

Jake, settled in his saddle, said, "B.J. says wait. And she's usually right."

"All the ladies say wait," Pete added. "Even Janie, and she's a rancher, even if she isn't a man. You know they're all smart. Give Lizzie a chance, Chad. She might surprise you."

"I hope you, and they, are right," Chad growled. Then he gathered the men working with him, and rode off.

Toby followed Pete and the twins. They were cutting steers out of a herd for the fall market. But his mind remained fixed on Elizabeth.

"YOU'VE SET UP a bachelor auction?" Abby Gaylord screamed.

Elizabeth shushed her. She didn't think anyone could hear, since the door was closed, but they were in school, after all. "Is that all right? I had to include the twins. Then the younger ones wanted to participate. You need to decide on an age limit. Someone suggested twenty-one for legal protection."

"But some of your cousins are in college. We'd make more money if we set it at eighteen. And of course it's okay. It will be an incredible success! Think of all the money we'll raise."

"Will someone agree to participate other than Randalls? We want something the entire community will like."

"Every single lady in the county will like it, which means every single man will love it. We'll have a huge turnout which will raise more money for the traditional booths like darts, cake walk, all kinds of things." Abby sprang to her feet and hugged Elizabeth. "You're a genius!"

Elizabeth hugged her friend, then shook her head. "No, I'm not, but I'm glad you're pleased."

Abby immediately drew out paper and began making lists. She was highly organized. "I'll check with the principal for an okay, then start handing out jobs. This is going to be great. Everyone in the county will start strategizing about who they want to purchase."

"Does that include you?" Elizabeth asked. Abby had certainly dated when she was in high school. And Elizabeth assumed she had in college. But since Elizabeth had returned, she hadn't heard any gossip about Abby's social life.

Abby grinned. "Why not? I haven't found anyone to fulfill my dreams, like you."

Cleve fulfill her dreams? If she'd ever considered her romantic dreams, maybe she would've known earlier he wasn't the one. All of Cleve's ideas seemed to be destined to fill his dreams, not hers.

Unfortunately, all her dreams were of Toby. And he wasn't interested.

She smiled at her friend. "If you need any help, let me know. You deserve someone special."

Abby shielded her gaze. "I might just do that, Elizabeth. Thanks." Then she hurried from the room.

Elizabeth frowned. Did Abby have a specific person in mind? Was it Toby? She'd been so enthusiastic about him yesterday. Elizabeth's heart sank. That wouldn't be easy to do. But Toby had to marry someone. Why not Abby? At least she'd fit in well with the family.

With a shrug, Elizabeth returned to her classroom. She was anxious for the week to end. She wanted to get Cleve out of her life. She wanted to reassure her father. This morning he'd glared at her several times at breakfast. Her mother had assured her everything was all right, but she wasn't satisfied.

Her students began entering the classroom. She put aside her problems to smile at them.

"Miss Randall!" Nancy Epperhart called, racing up to her desk.

"Yes, Nancy? What is it?"

"Guess what! My mommy's going to have a baby!"

"How exciting! When?"

"She said it would be my Christmas present! So I told her I wanted a sister." The little girl frowned.

"She said I was getting a brother. But I don't want a stinky boy. That's not fair since it's *my* present. Will you help me write a letter to Santa? He can keep his old boy. I'll take a dolly, instead."

Her personal problems disappeared and she began working on Nancy's.

WHEN FRIDAY AFTERNOON finally arrived, Elizabeth packed up the papers she needed to grade that weekend, ready to get her life on track. It had been a difficult time each evening as she faced her father's disapproval.

She'd been his pet, his only daughter, and she'd basked in his approval. She was definitely spoiled.

As she headed for her car, the school secretary stopped her. "Bill Johnson wants you to call him, Elizabeth."

"Oh, thanks, Millie. Um, I think I'll just stop by his office before I go home."

What could he want? She'd told him it would be this weekend before she talked to Russ about the accounting job. She hoped she hadn't been mistaken about Russ's interest. But they'd talked one evening, just the two of them, and she'd gotten the impression that Russ might like a job that didn't include cattle.

She parked in front of Bill's office and went in. "Bill? It's Elizabeth. Did you call?"

He met her at the door of his office, an eager expression on his face. "Yeah. Have you talked to Russ?"

"No," she said with a sigh. "First I have to talk to Cleve, you know. He's not here yet."

"So maybe tomorrow?"

She smiled. "Maybe. Do you need help that badly?"

"It wouldn't hurt. And I've got some more plans I want to discuss with him."

"I promise I'll talk to Russ as soon as I can. I'll have him call you. And I appreciate your patience." She gave him a smile and backed out of his office.

On the drive to the ranch, she gave thanks that Russ worked on the ranch and didn't go into town all that often. Otherwise, as eager as Bill was, Russ would've known by now.

And what if Russ had no interest? He'd always done well in accounting. He'd majored in it. But that didn't mean he'd want to do it all the time. Uncle Pete never showed any interest. Uncle Brett handled most of the numbers.

Oh dear, she might have upset everyone. Then her father would really be irritated with her.

There was no sign of Cleve's car when she reached the ranch. She'd hoped he'd be there early and she could send him on his way before dinner. But to brighten the day, she saw the SUV that Caroline drove. She'd come home to see Toby. Maybe Victoria and Jessica, Brett and Anna's daughters, had come with her.

The three girls, all her female cousins, were sitting in the kitchen with their mothers and aunts and Red and Mildred. Elizabeth was closest to Caroline, of course, because they were almost the same age, but all four of them did a lot together.

After hugs all around, Elizabeth sat beside Caroline and listened to their news.

Red added a little of his own. "Your friend called, said he'd be here about six-thirty, in time for dinner."

Drat! She'd have to eat with him. It would be rude to have Cleve drive all this way and not feed him. "Oh, uh, thanks, Red. I hope that's all right."

"A'course. We're not rude to guests." Mildred elbowed him. "What? I said I'd feed him."

Elizabeth smiled at Mildred. "It's fine, Mildred."

"So you're still engaged?" Caroline asked.

Elizabeth stared at her. Had she heard something? "Um, yes." But not much longer.

Much to her relief, Caroline didn't say anything else. She'd never cared for Cleve, which showed she was smarter about men than Elizabeth.

"How's Toby?" Caroline asked, her gaze still fixed on Elizabeth.

B.J. answered. "He's fine. I think he's really going to stay this time."

"I'm glad. Some of those articles I read about him make me think I don't know my brother anymore," Caroline complained. "It's time he gave me some nieces and nephews."

"And me a grandbaby," B.J. added softly.

"We'd all like to have some babies around here,"

Janie added. "Even Casey is getting too old for me to pretend he's my baby."

"Did Uncle Pete talk you into letting him move to the Pad?" Caroline asked, grinning.

Janie nodded, her expression not happy.

"Casey?" Victoria asked, her tone shocked. "He's still too— He's fourteen, isn't he? I remember I thought I was an adult then. I guess he deserves to move out."

Jessica protested. "When I moved to college three weeks ago, you protested, Mom, and I'm eighteen!"

"But you're a girl," Anna said, then looked guilty.

"Aha! I knew you and Dad favored boys."

"We do no such thing," Anna said, refusing to accept that accusation. "But—but we want you to be safe. Not all men are gentlemen, like the men in our family. Especially city boys."

"Don't worry, Mama Anna," Caroline said, leaning over to pat Anna's arm. "I'm keeping a good eye on them, and I'm giving them lessons on how to handle the bad ones."

"Thank you, Caroline," Anna said, while her children protested the need.

Because of all the noise of their conversation, Elizabeth didn't know Cleve had arrived early until he appeared at the back door. She drew a deep breath and stood to let him in.

"I came to the front door, but no one answered," he complained, frowning.

"I'm sorry," Elizabeth said. "We were talking and didn't hear your car."

He greeted the mothers and then said hello to Caroline and the two other girls. "I got here early," he said, as if she'd been dying for his return. "Want to go for a ride before dinner?"

For once, he'd pleased Elizabeth. She'd love to send him on his way at once, before her father returned to the house.

"Yes, thank you. You'll excuse us, Mother?"

"Of course, dear." There was a message in her mother's gaze that said she hoped Elizabeth would take care of everything.

She nodded and led her fiancé out of the house.

When they got in the car, she said, "Let's not go anywhere. I have something I have to say, and I don't want you driving while we talk."

"Sounds serious," Cleve said, but his voice held no concern. Either she didn't mean anything to him, and she kind of hoped that was it, or he had no idea what was going on.

"Oh," he said before she could speak, "by the way, I got a return call on a job in Denver. I'm supposed to interview with them on Monday. Aren't you pleased?"

"Uh, yes. When did you send in your application?"

"In June. They hired someone else, but that person didn't work out. Now they're interested in me."

"Didn't you tell me in June that you wanted to get

a job in Rawhide so we could be together?'' She knew he'd told her that. She'd been so impressed that he cared about her that much.

He shrugged his shoulders. ''The firm in Denver turned me down.''

Disgusted, she shook her head. ''I'm not going to Denver.''

''Of course you are. You go where your husband does. That's the way it goes.''

''Which means I'm not going to marry you.''

He laughed. ''Come on, babe, where are you going to find a better husband here? They're all a bunch of hicks who'll never go anywhere.''

She'd felt guilty, backing out of their engagement, but not now. ''Any of these hicks,'' she said softly, ''are honest and trustworthy, kind and gentle.'' Okay, she could remember a few who didn't fit those qualities, but most of them did.

''But they won't get anywhere in the world. I'm going to make a mark. And you'll be with me.''

''No, I won't.''

''Your father will disagree. He'll expect you to go with me. That's what women are supposed to do.''

''My father will celebrate if I dump you. I'm not going to marry you, Cleve. I realized it last Monday night. I tried to tell you on Tuesday morning, but you hurried back to Laramie. I waited until you came back to tell you in person, but I won't change my mind. You'd be very unhappy with me. And I'd be very unhappy with you. So, let's call it quits in a civil manner.''

He stared her. "You're serious? After me investing all this time and energy in you? We've been dating for almost six months!"

"I thought I—you were very nice."

"Of course I was. You wouldn't let me touch you! But I figured your family money would make it worthwhile!" he snapped.

"My family's money has nothing to do with me."

"Of course it does. We'll receive good gifts. Maybe a loan if we need it, and when they die—"

She reached for the door handle. "Go away. I don't ever want to see you again."

His hand grabbed hers as she tried to open the door. "Don't think you're going to walk away, lady. You owe me. I didn't even get sex out of you. I had to find ladies not so particular. I had to sneak around. I'm not letting you go without paying me something."

It didn't quite occur to Elizabeth what he was demanding as payment until he ripped her blouse half off her and grabbed one breast.

"What are you— Stop! No, don't touch me!"

He ignored her and hauled her against him, his mouth covering hers. She wrenched away and screamed. He slapped her across the face. She began fighting in earnest, realizing he intended to rape her. And she continued to scream.

THEY'D QUIT a little early because it was Friday night.
Chad still suspected something was going to happen
and he wanted to be there. And Jake was sure Caroline was coming in from school. And Brett figured
his girls would come with Caroline. And if they were
taking off early, so was everyone else.

Toby was in no hurry. He had no plans for Friday
night, even though the twins had asked him to go with
them to the local bar. He wasn't interested.

He'd rubbed down Cocoa and put away his gear,
waiting for the others to finish up, when he heard a
scream.

He didn't know how, but he recognized the scream
as Elizabeth's. Without any hesitation, he shoved
open the barn door just as a second scream ripped
through the air.

He hauled leather toward the house. Halfway there,
he heard her scream again and realized she was in the
front seat of a car.

He yanked open the door as he recognized the man
attacking her. Grabbing Elizabeth around the waist,
he pulled her out into his arms and immediately saw
the red stain on her cheek.

The back door of the house opened and several of
the women came out. He called to them to take care
of Elizabeth and rounded the car before the man inside could react. Toby pulled him out of the vehicle
and leveled his fist into the man's face.

Toby didn't speak. He followed Cleve down to the
ground and nailed him again. Any man who struck a

woman deserved to be beaten. Any man who beat Elizabeth had no right to live.

"Dad! Dad, stop him. Don't let him kill Cleve."

Hard hands seized his arms and shoulders, but he didn't stop. It angered him that Elizabeth would plead for the man when he'd tried to rape her. Did she love the animal that much?

"Toby! Son, stop, we'll call the sheriff. Back off." Jake's voice penetrated his murderous haze.

"He—" Toby tried to get out, still pulling against his father and uncles. "He was attacking Elizabeth!"

Toby turned his head to stare at her, to see if she was all right. She was surrounded by the women in the family.

Chad crossed to the group. "Elizabeth? Megan, is she all right?"

The other women stepped back, leaving Elizabeth, with Megan's arms around her, in front of her father. She had a bruise forming on one cheekbone, and her blouse hung from her body in shreds.

Chad took one look and turned to lunge for Cleve as he lay on the ground. Pete and Brett released Toby to his father's care and grabbed their brother.

"We'll take care of him, Uncle Chad," the twins and Jim and Josh shouted.

"Whoa!" Jake roared, bringing everyone to a halt. "We're not going to end up in jail. So no one is going to take advantage of the man. We're going to wait for the sheriff and press charges." Everyone stood there. He turned and looked at Elizabeth. "Right, Elizabeth?"

Toby waited tensely for her response. After all, she'd pleaded for Cleve, not him.

"Yes, Uncle Jake. I don't want any of you going to jail because of my stupidity."

"Good girl," Jake said with a grim smile. "Has anyone called the sheriff?"

"I did," B.J. said, smiling at her husband. "He's on his way."

"That's my girl."

Toby was glad his father was happy. He wasn't. He'd have liked to land a few more punches. And he'd have liked to have known for sure what Elizabeth was thinking. Would she regret that he came to her rescue? Or would she be grateful? And what was going to happen now?

Some women didn't handle violence well.

And how could he stand not taking her into his arms and reassuring her? Telling her he'd never let anyone hurt again? Because if he did that, he'd never let her go. And how could he face his dad and uncle then?

Chapter Six

Elizabeth felt like an idiot. It had never occurred to her that Cleve would react so violently. At her own home! Did he think she'd allow him to rape her without protest?

The sheriff took her inside for questioning, with only her mother beside her. She explained what had happened. The sheriff assured her she'd behaved as she should have. Then her mother had taken her upstairs.

She wanted to be there when the sheriff talked to Cleve...and to Toby. She wanted to make sure that no harm came to Toby for his rescue.

When her father came upstairs, and she heard the sheriff drive away, along with Cleve's car, Elizabeth met him at the top of the stairs.

"Did Toby get in trouble?"

"Nope, in spite of the man trying."

"You mean Cleve?"

"Yeah, he tried to convince the sheriff that he was

within his rights because you were his fiancée and you were refusing to have sex!''

Elizabeth stared at her father, stunned. "He said we were—were intimate?''

"Yeah," Chad said in disgust.

"We were not! Do you hear me, Dad? I never had sex with that man!''

Her father grinned. "I reckon the entire household hears you."

"Good. I want them to. Did the sheriff believe him?''

"Nope. He said you explained that you were still a virgin. He asked the jerk if he wanted you examined."

"Oh! How embarrassing!''

"Don't worry about it. He's being charged with attempted rape and assault and battery. I don't think you'll ever see him again."

"Good!''

"Why didn't you just tell him on the phone if you were getting rid of him?''

Megan grimaced at her husband. "Because that would be ill-mannered. You don't end a personal relationship by phone."

"So why didn't you tell me that?'' Chad demanded. "I've been worrying myself sick thinking she was going to elope."

Elizabeth gasped.

"I told you to trust her," Megan pointed out.

"Yeah, but—"

"I'm disappointed, Dad," Elizabeth said softly.

He shook his head. "I know, I know. I should've listened to your mother."

With a little smile, she kissed his cheek. "Or just trusted me to do what was right."

"I'm sorry you got hurt, Lizzie." He wrapped his arms around her. "Do you need to go to the doctor?"

"No. Is Toby okay?"

"Yeah. Mildred is patching up his hands, but he's fine. He's mad he didn't get in a few more punches."

Elizabeth hugged her dad tighter. "He's so strong I was afraid he'd hurt Cleve and be arrested."

"Nope, we're all free and clear with the sheriff. Your ex has troubles to deal with, but I expect he'll pay his bail and hightail it out of town."

"Good."

AFTER ANNOUNCING to her family that Cleve had lied, that she'd never slept with him, Elizabeth ate her dinner and retired to her room to read a novel. Then she slept well, better than she had in months.

When she came down to breakfast the next morning, several hours later than on weekdays, the men had been in the saddle quite a while. Saturday was a normal workday for them. She wanted to personally thank Toby for his rescue, but it seemed last night that he'd wanted to avoid her.

She did some schoolwork, preparing a game to teach the children their alphabet. She did her own laundry, even though her mother insisted the ladies who cleaned the ranch house could do it. She paid bills, visited with Caroline, and her other cousins Torie and Jessica.

But her interest picked up when she heard the men coming in from the stables. She rushed to the window in her bedroom, staring down at them as they approached the house.

"Everyone okay?" Caroline asked.

"Looks like it."

"What do you think about Toby?"

Elizabeth turned to stare at her cousin. "What do you mean?"

"How does he act around you?"

"He avoids me," she said solemnly. "He's friendly with the guys, but—he didn't like Cleve."

Caroline snorted. "Big surprise! No one but you liked him."

"How could I have been so blind?" Elizabeth wailed.

"He was nice to you."

"But—"

"You didn't ask much from him. I don't think you loved him."

"If I didn't love him, why would I agree to marry him?" she demanded.

Caroline sat silently, curled up on Elizabeth's bed. Then she looked at her cousin. "Because you don't expect to marry the man you love."

"What? That makes no sense!"

"I've tried to tell myself that. At first, I was even

happy about Cleve. Then I started watching you. And now I realize it makes perfect sense.''

Elizabeth plumped down in the nearby chair. ''What are you talking about?''

''I think you gave up on marrying for love when you were sixteen.'' Caroline watched her, sympathy in her gaze that bothered Elizabeth.

''That's ridiculous. I didn't even know what love was when I was sixteen.'' She stood up and walked back to the window. Everyone had gone inside.

''That's when you discovered that Toby had a girlfriend.''

''What does that have to do with anything?'' Elizabeth demanded, aware that her color was rising.

''Lizzie, I love my brother, but I don't *love* my brother. You do.''

''No! No, he's my cousin. I—I love him like a cousin. That's all. I wouldn't— It would be— You're wrong.'' She crossed her arms around her waist and backed away from Caroline.

Caroline pushed the pillow behind her back and waited. Then she said softly, ''Why are you backed into a corner?''

Elizabeth looked around her, realizing her cousin was right. She took a step forward. ''I don't know. But if you've known this for so long, why haven't you said anything?''

''I figured you'd work it out on your own. Then Cleve came along.''

Elizabeth hung her head, her eyes closed, as a huge

weight dropped from her shoulders. She'd been fighting her feelings without even realizing it for a long time. "But, we *are* cousins."

"Yes, but Mom says you're not blood cousins. She said it would be unusual, but nothing illegal, if you two married."

"You asked her?" Elizabeth asked in horror.

"Why not? I wanted to know if there was any hope."

"Wasn't she horrified?"

"Nope. She said you'd be a wonderful daughter-in-law and Toby would love his children having actual Randall blood."

With a gasp, Elizabeth said, "But Toby's not interested."

"I'm not sure. He's avoided us and home a long time for no good reason that I could see. What if he feels something for you but is afraid that it's bad?"

"You're being ridiculous!"

Caroline lifted one eyebrow. "Are you sure?"

"No," Elizabeth said breathlessly. "Yes! I'm sure. I know he's seen a lot of beautiful women. He won't have thought about me."

"I've heard you called beautiful, too."

"This is crazy, Caro. I won't listen to it." Elizabeth began pacing the room. "What are we going to do tonight?" she asked, trying to change the subject.

"How about we go into town? Hang out with the crowd, see if there are any new guys I might like."

Elizabeth grinned at her cousin. "You're never interested in new guys. You still have medical school to get through.''

''I know. But I should keep my eyes open. And maybe you'll prove me wrong and find someone you like better than my rotten brother.''

The challenge in Caroline's eyes and voice stirred Elizabeth. Okay, maybe her cousin had a point. It was time to test it out, to either prove her wrong, or figure out what to do about her situation. ''Okay, I'll go. Do you mind if I call Abby Gaylord and ask her to meet us?''

''Abby?''

''We teach school together.''

''Sure, why not? I always liked her. Tell her we'll meet her there in forty-five minutes. We can buy dinner there, but it'll take me that long to pretty up.''

''You've got a deal.

TOBY DREADED going to dinner. He figured Elizabeth would try to corner him again to thank him. She'd thanked him in front of the family last night, but he'd read the frustration in her eyes when he'd ducked the earlier attempts to get him alone.

Hell, he didn't want to be thanked. He was angry that they'd stopped him. He'd wanted to wipe off the man's face, to destroy him. She was his cousin. That was good enough reason for his reaction. His other cousins had offered to take up where he'd left off.

That's all it was. Defending his cousin.

Which left him an enormous difficulty. Now Elizabeth wasn't engaged. Wasn't about to be married, kept safe from his inappropriate feelings.

Damn, damn, damn. He was so glad to be back home. He didn't want to leave again. He wasn't ready to set up his own place. He wanted a little more time with his family. If he stayed, he'd have to keep his hands off Elizabeth. Could he do it?

He didn't know the answer to that question. He only knew he had to face her tonight.

When he entered the kitchen, the ladies were putting dinner on the table, its sides filling up with hungry Randalls. He looked for Elizabeth, only because he intended to avoid her, of course.

"Where's Elizabeth?" he demanded sharply. "Is she all right?"

His father grinned. "I guess so. She and Caroline went into town."

"What for?"

Everyone stared at him. Then Rich said, "What do you usually go into town for on a Saturday night, Toby? You haven't been gone so long that you've forgotten Saturday nights in Rawhide?"

Toby was stunned. She was practically raped yesterday, and she was heading into the meat market in Rawhide, where cowboys looked for ladies to share their evening with? Some of them with visions of dawn with the woman on the pillow next to them that they'd cut out of the herd.

Was she out of her mind?

"And you let her go?" Toby demanded of Chad.

"She's with your sister," Chad pointed out.

"You think Caroline is going to protect her?" Toby demanded, and his mother and father protested.

Toby turned around and headed to the back door, grabbing his hat off the rack.

"Where you going?" Russ demanded.

Toby turned around, ready to fire back his intention, that of protecting Elizabeth. With the stares, he decided to add Caroline's name. Then he decided not to be quite so specific. "I think I'll go into town this evening."

"But you said—" Russ began.

"I changed my mind," he snapped.

"Hang on, I'll go with you," Russ said and stood.

That suited Toby. He didn't want to be quite so obvious. "You, too, Rich?"

"Nope. I've already got plans with my lady. We're going to the movies."

"Fair enough. Sorry about dinner, Red," Toby added as he waved goodbye. He and Russ hurried out the door.

"Interesting," Jake muttered.

"Very," Chad agreed.

"I'M SO GLAD you called me," Abby said after sitting down at the table the two cousins had commandeered.

"I'm glad you could come," Elizabeth assured her.

"Me, too," Caroline added. "Catch me up with what's going on in your life."

They chatted a couple of minutes before the first cowboy stopped by the table. "Evenin', ladies."

"Hi, Larry," Caroline said. "Nice to see you."

"Aw, as pretty as you are, Caroline, you know I'm glad to see you. Your cousin done got herself engaged, and Abby won't have anything to do with me. So how about a dance?"

Caroline grinned. "I'll dance with you, but Elizabeth isn't engaged anymore, and Abby can be sweet-talked, just like the rest of us."

"I'll keep that in mind," the cowboy said, staring at the other two.

As they walked away toward the small dance floor, two more cowboys appeared. In no time, all three ladies were on the dance floor, doing the two-step.

IN THE DARKNESS of the cab of Toby's truck, Russ broke the silence. "You worried about Elizabeth?"

"Hell yes, I'm worried about Elizabeth. These cowboys can be pretty rough."

"Come on, Toby, they all know Elizabeth."

"Strangers come in sometimes." He stared straight ahead, driving fast.

"None of the guys would let anyone hurt her," Russ assured him.

Toby didn't respond. He didn't want to tell Russ he was afraid Elizabeth wouldn't want to be touched. That she might panic. And no one would understand. That he didn't want anyone to touch her...except him. To protect her, of course.

They reached the edge of town.

"Better slow down. Sheriff gives lots of speeding tickets. Not a good way to start the evening." Russ had himself braced, in case Toby threw on the brakes in a hurry.

He sighed as Toby took his advice. In a couple of minutes Toby parked near the bar where most of the singles in the area hung out. After all, there wasn't much to do at night in Rawhide. The picture show only offered one movie every two weeks.

Toby and Russ stepped to the sidewalk, two impressive figures that drew the eye, especially Toby with his rodeo fame. When they crossed to the entrance and moved past the cowboys smoking outside, there were murmurs following them.

"I think you're about to be recognized," Russ whispered beside him.

Toby could hear the excitement in his voice, but the idea of people wanting his autograph was old hat. He had other things on his mind.

"I can't see much. Have you found them yet?" he muttered at Russ.

"Who?" Russ asked, his gaze scanning the room.

"The girls, of course!"

"Hey! It's Toby!" a cowboy called from the bar. A mad rush of men and women started, wanting to shake his hand, ask for an autograph, and, most of all, press the flesh. The women in particular kissed his cheek, his lips if they were very bold, or asked for a hug.

Toby tried to be patient, but over their heads he kept looking for Elizabeth. He figured she'd be sitting against the wall, half hiding from the sharks that cruised the room looking for women without dates.

But he couldn't find her.

Then, one of his friends from his youth stepped away, leaving an opening that showed the dance floor. There, in a cowboy's arms, was Elizabeth, throwing her head back and laughing.

Toby stepped forward, closely followed by the crowd. Why wasn't this cowboy rushing to shake his hand? With a rueful smile, he reminded himself he wouldn't choose shaking a rodeo star's hand over holding Elizabeth.

"Listen, handsome," one of the women whispered. "I've got a free dance when you're ready."

"Thanks. I'll keep that in mind. Excuse me," he added as he moved forward again. Breaking free, he reached out and tapped the cowboy's shoulder. "My turn."

An old friend turned around. "Why, Toby. Welcome back,"

"Hi, Joe. Mind if I cut in?"

"I sure do! She's been engaged until tonight. Why would I want to share her with her cousin?" the man asked, grinning.

"Because if you don't," Toby said, smiling grimly, "I'm going to ram your tongue down your throat."

His friend looked a little startled, then relented.

"Plenty of dances to go around, Tobe. No need to get violent."

Elizabeth, who'd said nothing so far, smiled at Joe. "I'll save you the next one."

"All right, darlin'," Joe agreed, looking happier.

Toby slid his arm around Elizabeth's small waist and moved her away.

"Why did you do that?" she demanded in a whisper.

"Do what?"

"Stop Joe from dancing with me? He's a nice guy and a friend of yours."

"I have a better question. Why are you dancing with people after what happened to you last night?"

"These are my friends. They wouldn't hurt me," Elizabeth protested.

He frowned even more deeply. "Damn it! Why do you want to dance with them? Why couldn't you just stay put, rest, hell, I don't know, join a nunnery or something?"

Elizabeth stopped in the middle of the dance floor, her hands on her hips, which only drew notice to the short denim skirt that fit her snugly.

"Damn, are you trying to drive men crazy, tempting them?" he demanded, moving forward to take hold of her again.

She struck at his hands, turned and left the dance floor.

Toby swore he'd never understand women, but he followed her through the crowd, ignoring those who hadn't spoken to him yet and wanted him to stop a minute.

When he finally reached the table, his cousin Russ was sitting there, talking to Abby and Elizabeth.

"Hey, Toby, did you notice they refinished the dance floor?" Russ asked. "It's nice, isn't it?"

Toby stared at him. "No. I didn't notice."

"He's too busy trying to run everyone's lives," Elizabeth put in. "He thinks I should join a nunnery."

Abby stared at him. "Why?"

Russ, too, seemed dumbfounded. "Yeah, why?"

"I just thought she ought to give herself time to— to adjust to—she had a tough time last night!"

"Toby, I'm not fragile. And I won't let Cleve make me afraid of my own shadow."

"Not afraid, honey, but a little slower to get back to the water trough." Toby thought he'd put that delicately enough. But apparently Elizabeth didn't.

She glared at him. "If you're going to sit at our table, stay out of my business."

Since Joe, with the new music starting, appeared at her side, she said nothing else until she'd stood and taken Joe's hand. "You'll excuse me, won't you, Toby?"

He saw the line drawn in the sand. "Sure. You two enjoy yourselves. I'll wait right here."

And that was where he drew his own line.

Chapter Seven

Elizabeth had always seen Toby as her hero, her protector, her...whatever. She wasn't feeling quite so appreciative now. By the time the evening ended, she was ready to slug him if he even spoke to her.

She'd never danced so much in her life, but she accepted every invitation just to show Toby Randall he couldn't run her life. So it was his fault she thought she was rubbing a blister with her new boots.

"Finally ready to go?" Toby asked, glaring at her, his hands on his hips. "Or did you want to spend the night here?"

"What difference does it make to you? You have your truck. You can go home whenever."

"Come on, Lizzie," Caroline intervened. "You know he's trying to take care of you. Give him a break."

"It's amazing how I managed the past six years while he was away earning fame and fortune, hanging out with all those models!"

Russ and Abby left the dance floor as the last song

ended and arrived at the table. "Ready to go?" Russ asked.

"I think so if we can get these two to stop fighting," Caroline said with a chuckle. "Maybe I'll ride with you so they can sort things out."

Elizabeth wasn't about to agree to that. But she didn't have a good reason until Russ called goodnight to someone named Bill. This nudged her memory about the job with Bill Johnson. She couldn't believe she'd forgotten to tell Russ at once to call the accountant.

"Oh! Oh, Russ I have to talk to you. You come ride with me and Toby can see Caroline home." She assumed they'd all agree and started toward the door.

"Ride with my brother?" Caroline protested. "He'll give me the third degree!"

"I'm serious," Elizabeth promised her cousin. "I was supposed to have Russ call—call someone. I promise."

Caroline accepted her excuse and managed to get them all outside to the vehicles. Toby stared at Elizabeth as she slipped behind the wheel.

"We'll follow you," he growled, as if he expected her to run away from home.

"Right," she agreed and shut the door. But she couldn't leave yet. Russ was saying goodbye to Abby. Elizabeth frowned. She'd thought Abby was interested in Toby, but after initially greeting him, Abby hadn't paid much attention to him tonight. Of course, who would? He'd been a real bear. He hadn't danced even once after he'd interrupted her dance with Joe.

Russ opened the door and slid in. "Want me to drive or are you okay?"

Elizabeth grimaced. "Don't pull the Toby routine, Russ. He's driven me crazy tonight." She put the car in gear and pressed on the gas.

Russ looked over his shoulder to see Toby pull in behind them. "Looks like he's still doing it."

"I know. Did you and Abby—I mean, you sure talked a lot tonight."

"Haven't seen her in a while," he said casually, but Elizabeth noticed he stared out the window, averting his gaze.

"We teach together, you know."

"Yeah, she told me all about the bachelor auction and how you came up with the idea."

"She looked pretty tonight," Elizabeth added, watching him closely.

"She always has."

Finally, she gave up the subtle approach. "Are you going to ask her out?"

He appeared startled. "Look, I just came along with Toby to make sure he didn't—he was upset that you went out."

Elizabeth's eyebrows soared. "That's ridiculous! There's no reason I shouldn't go to town."

Russ shrugged his shoulders. "Is that what you wanted to talk to me about?"

She'd forgotten again. "No. No, but I promised Bill Johnson you'd call him."

"Bill Johnson? Why?"

"You know Cleve was going to join his firm, only it didn't work out. And—and I told him you might be interested."

Russ stared at her, confusion on his face.

In the truck behind, Toby was trying to talk to his sister.

"Caro, this was a crazy idea. Why did you suggest it?"

"You'd prefer that she sat home and felt miserable?" Caroline asked, her eyebrows raised. "She didn't love him, and I didn't want him to make her feel bad."

"Of course not, but—I've tried to teach both of you to be on guard."

"She will be. But you're not always going to be around. She has to learn to take care of herself. She was fighting last night. You saved her quickly, but I think she would've saved herself eventually."

Toby grunted, his gaze on the car in front of them. His sister's next question caught him off guard.

"Why did you decide to come home?"

He shrugged his shoulders. "I was tired of the rodeo life."

"It didn't have anything to do with Elizabeth's engagement?"

"Why would you ask that?"

"I've always thought you were partial to Elizabeth."

Toby slowed down and stared at his sister. "You think I prefer her to you?"

"Don't be silly, Toby. Look, I've had a lot of psychology classes and I think—"

Toby groaned. "I should've guessed. You can take your theories from psych class and write a novel or something. I don't need your ridiculous ideas just because I want you girls safe."

"But, Toby—"

"No, I don't want to hear it. Now, tell me how your classes are going."

He kept a steady conversation going with his sister, his gaze steadily fixed on Elizabeth, until they reached home.

ELIZABETH was still angry with Toby. When he'd protected her in the past, when she'd been a young girl, the threats had been real, if not life-threatening. But he hadn't interfered in her choices. Last night, he'd tried to keep her from dancing with anyone! So, of course, she'd danced with everyone.

She might have missed him, but she wasn't going to encourage such macho behavior. She came down, dressed for church in a demure suit, prepared to snub him.

He wasn't there.

"Is Toby sleeping in?" she asked after she was seated. At their age, most of the kids didn't have a curfew on Saturday night. But they were expected to be at the breakfast table dressed for church on Sunday morning.

"He's gone," Russ said as he served himself some eggs.

"What?" Elizabeth demanded, her voice higher than she intended. "You mean he went back to the rodeo?"

B.J. provided the answer. "Just for a few days. One of his friends called, wanted to buy Cocoa. Toby didn't feel he could sell his horse, but he agreed to lend him to his friend for a few days. He's staying with him to be sure Cocoa is all right."

"Oh." It was as if the sun had set. All her enthusiasm for the day was gone. She had nothing to look forward to. Toby wasn't here. And maybe he wouldn't come back. After coming home and finding how boring it could be here, he might change his mind. Stay at the rodeo.

"You don't think he'll stay, do you?"

At first Elizabeth thought she'd said those words. Then she realized her voice wasn't a deep boom. It was Jake who'd said that.

B.J. kept her eyes on the eggs she was eating but said quietly, "I don't know. He said he'd be back next weekend."

Rich looked up from his breakfast. "I guess Cocoa is almost as famous as Toby. He's had some outrageous offers to buy him."

"A good horse can make a difference," Pete said.

"I was thinking about telling him he should start training horses to sell. He'd make good money. It'd help pay the bills for him when the price of beef is down."

"Hey, that's right! Good idea, Pete. I'd forgotten he trained Cocoa himself," Jake said, smiling again.

"Isn't he leaving you in a lurch, going off without notice?" Elizabeth asked, her voice stiff.

The older men looked up, stared at her and then each other. Finally Jake answered. "We told him if he changed his mind, it was all right, Elizabeth. But he asked me before he decided to go. I won't hold a child of mine who doesn't want to be at home. That's why we let him go in the first place."

She knew that. But it didn't make it any easier to bear that Toby was gone. She wanted him back. She'd had four or five days with him back in her life. She might've gotten irritated with him, but she missed him.

Her mother reached over and took her hand as it rested in her lap. "I'm sure he'll be back. I was in the kitchen when he took the call. He wasn't excited about going back. The friend had to beg him to help. It seems the friend is on the trail to the nationals. His horse will only be out this week, but he'll miss a lot of points if he doesn't perform."

"I'm sure Toby couldn't refuse in those circumstances," Jake said.

"Yeah, or people would say he was jealous," Josh added. "Though no one would believe it!"

Several agreed with Toby's little brother.

Red got up from the table. "You all still eating? You'd better hurry or we'll all be late."

Soon Toby's circumstances were forgotten by most of them as they filled several vehicles for the trip to the local church, where Randall marriages usually took place.

Elizabeth caught a ride with her parents, but her thoughts remained on Toby. In church she added a special prayer for his return.

TOBY LEANED AGAINST the rails of the corral, watching Lonnie practice roping the calf. When his friend had dismounted, bound three of the calf's legs and thrown his hands in the air, he clicked the stopwatch.

"How'd I do?" Lonnie hollered across the arena.

"Good. Five-point-seven."

Lonnie threw his hands in the air. "You know that won't win me much."

"Depends." He watched his friend stride to the fence, leading Cocoa.

"What can I do?"

Toby debated how much to say. Finally, he cleared his throat. "Well, you're wasting time telling Cocoa what to do. He'll take care of his job so you can tend to yours."

"What do you mean?"

Toby began to detail how Cocoa was trained. He'd trained his horse to be his best partner.

When he finished, Lonnie gave a nod of comprehension and headed back to try again.

"Hi, cowboy. You lonesome?" a silky soprano voice said. Turning around, Toby found an old friend at his elbow. "Hi, Sally. Long time no see. How's Wes?"

Sally was a barrel rider married to one of the bronc riders. She'd been following the rodeo for more than ten years.

"I wouldn't know. We separated about a month ago, just before you pulled out. Are you back?"

"Just temporarily." He was caught by a shout from Lonnie. "Ready!" he yelled in return and clicked the stopwatch.

Sally stood silently beside him as they watched Lonnie rope another calf and tie it up.

"Better," Toby called when Lonnie turned to look at him. "Five-two. And that calf fought you a little. Good job."

"I'm going again!" Lonnie said, a smile on his face.

Toby nodded.

"I'm looking for a partner," Sally said, surprising him. "You interested?"

That question brought his attention back to the woman beside him. "Uh, I'm going back home at the end of the week."

"Why? Why did you leave rodeo in the first place?" Sally asked.

"I was tired of this life. I missed my family." He

wouldn't have had the nerve to say that when he was younger. But now he knew what was important.

Sally slid her arms around his neck. She was a beautiful woman, strong and fit. Many considered her the best-looking woman on the circuit. "I could be your family."

Toby held back his laughter. He didn't want to hurt her feelings. "Sally, honey, you're a beauty, and you know it. Half the cowboys here would fall down at your feet if you just smiled at them. But I've got a huge family, and I want to be with them. I can't stay…even for you."

"I don't want just anyone. I want you. I've always wanted you. That's why Wes was never very friendly to you. He knew how I felt."

Toby was appalled. What kind of hell was that, married to a woman who wanted someone else? He took hold of her arms and lowered them from his neck. "I'm sorry, Sally, but I'm going home."

"Must be a girl there."

"Maybe." He'd been trying to do some thinking about that situation while he was away.

"Ready?" Lonnie called.

Toby waved and clicked the stopwatch as Lonnie urged Cocoa after the calf. He kept his eyes on his friend, but he felt Sally drift away. He was glad. He'd been approached by several women since he'd gotten back. Whether for a night or for a year or two, they'd all offered to take him in and provide some entertainment, too.

He'd turned them all down. Clicking the time when Lonnie finished, he called, "Four-nine. Now you're cookin'."

Around five o'clock, when he figured Elizabeth would be home, he called the ranch.

ELIZABETH had just gotten a cup of coffee and headed for a seat at the table when the phone rang. "I'll get it," she called to Red. After all, she was already standing.

"Randall Ranch," she said.

"Elizabeth?"

"Yes, who—"

"It's Toby. Have you forgotten me already?"

"No, of course not. How are you?" she asked, turning her back to the others, in particular, B.J. Once she discovered it was her son on the phone, she'd want to talk to him.

"How's everything at the ranch?"

"Fine. They brought in the herd of steers you were rounding up yesterday. The brothers were pleased." That was how the second generation referred to the original four Randalls.

"Good."

"How—how are things there?"

"Good. Lonnie placed last night in both events. He's thrilled with Cocoa, of course. Wants me to train him a horse."

"Uncle Pete was talking about that on Sunday."

"He was?"

"Yes, he thinks you should make it a business," she said. Probably she should have left this conversation to Pete, but she wanted to give Toby a reason to come home.

"Good idea. How are your classes?"

"Fine." Then she remembered something he might be interested in. "Russ is thinking about working with Bill Johnson in town a few hours a week."

"Really? What brought that on?"

"Uh, I did. I thought he wanted something else to do besides the ranch work and he's always been good with numbers."

"So he's happy with it?"

"I think so."

"That really leaves the brothers shorthanded. I'd better hurry back."

Elizabeth almost cheered out loud. She wanted him to have lots of reasons to come back.

"Are you still mad at me?"

His soft question grabbed her heart. "No, not really, but I'm old enough to make my own decisions."

"I just wanted you safe."

"I know," she agreed with a sigh. "Are you coming home?"

He sounded surprised. "Of course. This weekend. Didn't someone tell you?"

"I thought you might discover you missed rodeo."

The pause before he responded killed her. She forgot to breathe until he said, "No. I miss being *there*."

Elizabeth drew a deep breath. A noise behind her

reminded her she'd better hand the phone over to B.J. or her name would be mud. "Did you want to speak to your mom?"

"Is she there?"

"Yes." She put her hand over the mouthpiece and called, "B.J.? It's Toby."

"Elizabeth?" Toby called as she put her ear to the phone.

"Yes?"

"I just wanted to say I miss you. I'll be home soon."

"Okay. Here's your mom." And she handed the receiver to B.J. But his special goodbye to her was more than enough to put a smile on her face. Toby was coming home.

"What did the boy say?" Red asked anxiously.

"He's coming home," she assured him, the smile still on her face. She knew that was what Red wanted to know. "His friend is doing well. He's placed in both events, I guess steer wrestling and calf roping. And he wants Toby to train a horse for him. I told him what Pete said about starting a business."

"Good. Give him something to think about," Red agreed, nodding.

B.J. hung up the phone and came back to the table. "He sounds good, and he's definitely coming back." She was beaming.

"Lizzie told us," Mildred said.

It was just the four of them at the table. Janie was

at her mother's ranch, Megan at her store in Rawhide and Anna was working a few hours for Doc.

"Jake will be relieved," B.J. confessed. "He hasn't wanted to admit it, but he was afraid Toby would decide to stay."

"Lots of women around the rodeo," Red mumbled under his breath.

Elizabeth jerked her head up and stared at him. It wasn't that she didn't know about the women, but she hadn't thought about them in terms of Toby.

B.J. laughed. "I asked him about that, but he wouldn't talk about anything. He just said not to worry, he was coming home."

"What kind of women?" Elizabeth asked. Silly question. She knew what kind of women. What she meant was what kind of women Toby would be interested in.

B.J. and Red exchanged a look that Elizabeth didn't understand.

"Lots of barrel racers, workers, you know, those kind of women," Red said. "He used to tell me—" He stopped abruptly when Mildred elbowed him. "What?"

"There are always lots of women," B.J. said, "especially around men like Toby...or any of the Randalls. We're all spoilt having them here, honey," she said to Elizabeth. "Look at the difference between them and Cleve. Any woman would choose one of them."

Elizabeth drew a deep breath. "Yes, of course, but since I'm family, it makes it a little more difficult."

Again the others looked at each other and said nothing. "Anyway," Elizabeth said, hoping to cover the awkward moment, "he's coming home."

"Here's hopin' he don't bring no buckle bunny home with him," Red added, but was again shushed by his wife.

Elizabeth excused herself and hurried up the stairs to her room. Good heavens, she hadn't thought about that happening since he came home this time. The thought that Toby might bring home a woman—a wife or fiancée—was devastating. But B.J. was right. She couldn't imagine any woman passing Toby by. His good looks and broad-shouldered, slim-hipped body would always draw a woman's eye. But his mind, his heart, oh, those were the best parts of Toby Randall. He was a true-blue gentleman, warm and caring.

And, she finally admitted to herself, she wanted him. Caroline's talk had pierced her denial. Given a choice—Toby or anyone else in the world—she didn't hesitate to say Toby. She was a little confused with her memories and the reality of Toby now. She could almost say she didn't know him. And yet she did. Most importantly of all, she didn't want to do without Toby in her life.

Now, the only question was how was she going to get him? And would her family approve?

Chapter Eight

Abby dropped by the teacher's lounge at lunchtime Friday.

"I'm thinking about going into Casper tomorrow to do a little shopping. Are you interested in going with me?"

Elizabeth had been composing a list of ways to attract Toby's attention. She looked up, her eyes sparkling. "Yes! Of course. Why didn't I think of that?"

Abby looked a little confused. "Think of shopping? I don't know. Why didn't you?"

"Um, I mean, I should upgrade my wardrobe." Elizabeth didn't want to confess what she was doing.

"Your wardrobe looks fine to me. I like that jumper."

"But it makes me look—like a kindergarten teacher."

"Ye-esss," Abby said slowly. "Aren't you a kindergarten teacher?"

"Yes, but I want to appear more exciting."

"To the kids?"

"No! Of course not. I mean I want to appear more exciting when I'm not teaching."

Abby sat down at the table, nodding her head. "I've got it now. There's a man whose attention you want to attract."

Elizabeth turned bright red. "How did you know?"

"Because that's the way I feel, too. Why do you think I'm going shopping?"

"Really? Who?"

"I'll tell if you will."

The frightening thought entered Elizabeth's head that they might be trying to attract the same man. She stared at her friend, looking for a clue to the identity of the man holding her interest.

"Maybe—maybe we shouldn't tell," she finally said, looking away. "It might jinx us," she added with a smile that took a lot of effort.

"Will it help if I tell you it's not Toby?" Abby asked, a rueful smile on her face.

"It's not? Oh," Elizabeth said as she let out a long sigh. "Are you sure? You were excited that he was coming back."

"Elizabeth, if everyone who was excited about Toby coming home wanted to marry him, the line would go from here to Casper. I'll admit I was interested. But—well, I ran into someone else and—"

"Russ?"

Abby's cheeks bloomed and she chewed on her bottom lip. "Was I that obvious?"

"No, not at all. I just thought you got along real well the other night."

Abby smiled, her gaze unfocused. "We did. We always have, but—I hadn't spent much time with him since high school, and usually Rich is around and he leads Russ away. He doesn't want Russ to tie himself up."

Elizabeth was taken aback by Abby's words. "Do you think so? I hadn't noticed that."

"I suppose it's hard with twins. You're always together, so being apart is—is difficult."

"Hmm. That would make it difficult on the girlfriend, too, wouldn't it?"

"Yeah, or the girlfriend-hopeful. Saturday night was the first time I'd seen Russ without Rich in years."

"But he had Toby with him."

"Yeah, but Toby was totally focused on you. Russ could've eloped with five ladies and Toby would never have known it."

"No, he wasn't that bad. He was upset with me."

"Duh. It wouldn't take a rocket scientist to know that. What did you do that had upset him? Surely, he was glad you broke up with Cleve? We all were."

"Cleve was a little heavy-handed about the breakup. He tried to—well, Toby stopped him, but he thought I should've stayed home and not spoken to men for a number of years, apparently."

"Ah, the nunnery comment."

"Yes. And I was angry with him about that. But before we could work it out, he left."

"He's gone? I hadn't heard that. Why didn't you tell me?"

Elizabeth sighed. "Because it's supposed to be temporary. He's due back Sunday evening. He took his horse to Denver to loan him to a friend for the week and stayed to take care of him."

"Oh, good. Gee, Denver. They've got great shopping in Denver. Too bad we couldn't— Hey! What if we flew to Denver tomorrow from Casper, shopped all day, got up the next morning and caught a ride back with Toby?"

Elizabeth's eyes widened. "It would be fun, but I don't *have* to go to Denver to shop. People might consider it a little over the top."

"So what? I've got money saved that I can use. And we all know the Randalls can afford it. Besides a one-way flight to Denver won't run that much."

Elizabeth felt excitement creep in. Why not? She was careful with money, but she had a little savings, too. Would Toby hate bringing them back? He had a double cab in his truck. "We'll have to call Toby and see if he minds," she said, her mind sorting through the things they'd have to do, "and call the airport to see if we can get seats and what time we'd have to get there."

"I'll call about the flight and you call Toby," Abby said. "There's another phone in the office. I'll go use it." Abby was out the door before Elizabeth could change her mind.

Elizabeth didn't have Toby's cell-phone number, so she called the ranch. By the noise she heard when Red answered the phone, she gathered the men, or at least some of them, had come in for lunch. She explained that she needed B.J., only to discover she was out on a vet case.

She almost left word and hung up, but then she had an inspiration. "Is Russ there?"

"Sure, honey. Hang on. Russ, telephone."

Her cousin answered the phone, and she told him about Abby's idea, adding that she needed to talk to Toby to see if he'd bring them home. Then she added, "You want to come, too?"

He didn't say anything, but Elizabeth didn't rush him.

After a minute, he said, "It sounds like fun, but I'm not sure I can take off. What? Uh, just a minute, Elizabeth." He covered the receiver with his hand. Then he came back on the line. "Dad says I can have the day off. Why don't I call Toby and check it out? Oh, and can you get me a seat on the plane? Abby won't mind, will she?"

Elizabeth grinned. "No, I don't think so, but we'll be shopping. So be warned."

"No problem. I'll talk to you when you get home."

"Okay, Russ. Thanks." She hung up the phone and sped down the hall to the office. Abby was still on the phone and she tapped her on the shoulder and held up three fingers.

"What?" Abby whispered.

"Make it three seats on the plane."

With a questioning frown, Abby reserved three seats. After hanging up, she said, "Why three? Who's going with us?"

"Who else? Russ!"

Abby's eyes glistened. "Russ? How did you pull that off?"

"Just remember you owe me one," Elizabeth told her, linking her arm with Abby's. "We're going to have an exciting weekend!"

THEY PICKED UP Abby at five-thirty the next morning in Russ's truck. Elizabeth claimed she might get sick if she didn't sit by the window, putting Abby between her and Russ. Elizabeth decided she was getting good at this romance thing, at least for someone else.

Once they were settled and on the road to Casper, she told Abby about Toby's response to their request. "He was pleased, according to Russ. He's taking us to dinner tonight and then to the last night of the rodeo. We get to see the finals."

"You're kidding. That's great! Are you pleased, Russ?"

"Yeah," he agreed with a smile, sparing her a look. "You bet. We won't get to see Toby perform, but we can watch Cocoa."

"And all the other performers," Elizabeth added. "Lots of cute guys, right, Abby?"

Abby stared at her friend as if she'd lost her mind. "What?"

But Elizabeth had her gaze on Russ and she noticed his concern. Yep, she was good at this.

"You interested in a rodeo star?" Russ asked, frowning.

Abby spoke slowly, as if picking her way through a minefield. "I like to watch them perform, but I'm not interested personally. I think it would be difficult to d-date one. They're never in one place for any length of time."

"Good point," Russ said, his body more relaxed. "I guess that's the reason Toby hasn't settled on a wife yet. He's going to be twenty-eight in October. He needs to think about the future."

Like a chorus, both women said, "He does?"

"Well, he hasn't said that, but I reckon that's why he's tired of rodeoing."

Elizabeth was torn between hoping Russ was right and worrying that he was. What if Toby started looking for a wife before she could catch his eye?

She was fully occupied worrying about her future until they reached the airport in Casper and boarded a small plane to fly down to Denver.

When they started shopping, she expected Russ to find other things to do. He could go to the rodeo grounds, or do his own shopping. Instead, he said he didn't really have much to shop for, so he was available to carry their packages if they wanted.

Elizabeth left the response up to Abby, knowing what her choice would be. In fact, Abby consulted Russ so often, Elizabeth could completely focus on her own wardrobe.

They broke for a late lunch. Already, they had a number of packages. After they were seated and had ordered their food, Russ suggested he run across the street to the hotel and put their purchases with the concierge where they'd left their bags earlier.

They were going to check into the hotel before they went to dinner. With Abby and Elizabeth's approval, he loaded all the bags into his arms and hurried out.

"Isn't he a delight?" Abby said with a sigh, a big smile on her lips.

Elizabeth grinned. "An absolute angel."

Abby blushed. "You're teasing me."

"Just a little. Russ is a good guy. Maybe not as perfect as you think, but he is a Randall, after all," she added, thinking of B.J.'s words again. "They're head and shoulders above most of the male population."

"And you're not prejudiced at all," Abby teased.

"Maybe a little, but after Cleve, we both know I've sampled the dregs of the human race. I can't believe I was so blind as to think I could marry that man."

"At least you woke up in time."

Before the conversation could continue, the waiter arrived with their lunch.

"Russ's hamburger will get cold if he doesn't hurry," Abby worried, staring out the window that looked down on their hotel.

"It won't be the first time Russ has eaten cold food," Elizabeth assured her friend. "I guess that will change for him if he works for Bill Johnson."

"Is he going to?" Abby asked, surprised. "I haven't heard anything about him changing jobs."

"You should ask—oh, here he is."

Russ, a smile on his face, rejoined them. Elizabeth decided he put his chair a little closer to Abby's this time.

"I'm glad you're back," Abby said with a beautiful smile that seemed to impress Russ. "I didn't want your food to get cold."

"No problem. It looks good."

Elizabeth wasn't sure he'd even looked at the food. He kept staring at Abby.

She cleared her throat to get his attention. "Abby and I were wondering if you'd come to any agreement with Bill."

He rubbed his chin. "We're thinking about it. He wants me to start off working half a week, see how it works out."

"You mean you'll be in town all day?" Abby asked. "Why, you could even have lunch with—with Elizabeth," Abby said hurriedly, her cheeks turning red.

Elizabeth was sure Abby's red cheeks meant she'd been thinking of herself as Russ's lunch partner.

"Yeah, I hadn't thought of that."

The other two continued to discuss the possibilities of the change in Russ's life and Elizabeth played with her food. Their enjoyment of each other's company made her feel a little lonely. And a little envious. She'd shared a meal with Toby many a time in her life, but not much as adults, and almost always in a crowd. A crowd of family. She'd never had a dinner conversation with him. She'd never been the focus of his attention, the way Abby was Russ's.

Except for last Saturday night, and that hadn't been pleasant. He'd wanted to skin her alive, not chat her up.

What about tonight? Would he talk to her the way Russ was talking to Abby? She hoped so.

"Elizabeth? Are you not hungry? We need to start shopping again if we're going to get finished," Abby said some minutes later.

"Oh! Yes, of course." She looked down at her plate and realized she'd only nibbled a few French fries. Picking up half her sandwich, she put it on Russ's plate. "You'd better eat that, Russ, because I won't have time for it."

She had to find something to wear that would ensure that Toby would notice her.

TOBY TOLD HIMSELF he shouldn't be excited about the evening, but he was. Instead of having Elizabeth with him as part of a crowd, it would just be the four of them. And he was pretty sure Russ was interested in

Abby. Not that he blamed him. Abby was a pretty, young woman and well-suited to his cousin.

So he'd have Elizabeth to himself. He'd have to be careful and not stay too focused on her. She wouldn't like it. But he could show her around and talk to her, just the two of them, without fighting. Last Saturday night had been a fight.

Tonight would be a pleasure.

He spent part of the afternoon cleaning out his truck. Then he showered and shaved again, polished his dress boots and put on clean clothes.

He ran into Lonnie before he could escape.

"Wow! You're all spiffed up. Is this to celebrate my win tonight?"

"Nope, and you'd better not be too cocky. You haven't won yet," he reminded his friend.

"You are coming to watch, aren't you?" Lonnie asked, sudden anxiety on his face. "You've been here every night this week."

"I'll be there. Some cousins came into town and we're going to dinner. Then all of us are coming back here to root you on."

"Whew, good. You had me worried there for a minute." Lonnie started to walk away. Then he stopped and asked, "Are any of those cousins of the female persuasion?"

Toby didn't want to answer that question because he knew what was coming next. "Uh, yeah."

"Hey, if I win, we'll party afterwards, okay?"

"We'll see. They've been shopping all day and they might be too tired."

"How old are your cousins?" Lonnie asked, staring at him.

Another question he didn't want to answer. And he didn't. Waving his hand, he hurried toward his truck. He didn't want to share Elizabeth with all the cowboys he knew. They'd all want to join them once they saw her.

He was picking them up at the hotel. Since there was no parking in front, Russ had told him they'd meet him downstairs. He pulled into the driveway, hoping they didn't keep him waiting. He caught sight of Russ at once, with Abby beside him. Then he saw Elizabeth.

She was standing apart from Abby and Russ, talking to a man in a suit. Dressed all in turquoise, from her tight-fitting western pants to her long-sleeved shirt; the color alone with her auburn hair would've made her stand out. But the snug fit would draw a man's attention, too. She'd left the top three shirt buttons undone, which left an intriguing hint of what was underneath the silk. To top it all, her hair, usually worn in a sedate plait or pulled back in a ponytail, was riotously curling down her back and about her face. She looked like a cowboy's goddess.

And Toby didn't like it at all.

Taking her to the rodeo like that would be like taking a mountain of cheese into a mouse stronghold and hoping to go unnoticed.

Russ saw him and waved. Then he took Abby's arm and stepped over to Elizabeth, pointing out Toby's arrival.

The man in the business suit seemed reluctant to let Elizabeth go. Not that Toby was surprised. It was a wonder the man hadn't thrown her over his shoulder and run. Frustration filled Toby.

He opened the door across from him to let them know he was ready to go. Still, it took several minutes to get Elizabeth away from the stranger. At least Toby hoped he was a stranger.

Finally the threesome reached the truck. Then Elizabeth suggested Russ sit up front because he'd have more leg room. Toby figured he'd kill Russ in his sleep tonight if he did that. Toby wanted Elizabeth in the front seat beside him so he could question her about the man who'd hung onto her so tightly.

Finally Russ helped Abby into the back seat and followed her, leaving Elizabeth to the front seat.

Before she'd even closed the door, he demanded, "Who was that man?"

Her eyebrows slid up and she stared at him. "What man?"

"The one you were talking to. I didn't know you knew anyone in Denver."

"As it so happens, I know several people in Denver." She paused and smiled at him. "Not that man, however. He stopped because he figured I was going to the rodeo and he wanted to ask me about it. He's thinking about going."

"Yeah, *now* he is," Toby muttered under his breath.

"What did you say?" she asked.

"Nothing. You didn't tell him your name, did you?"

"Of course not."

She didn't say anything else, and Toby wasn't sure what to say. He was afraid if he commented on her appearance, he'd start drooling. Or sound angry. He was going to have a hell of a night trying to keep her safe from a lot of cowboys.

"I, uh, hope steaks are all right. I made us reservations at a steak house near the rodeo. It's supposed to be good."

"Great," Russ responded. "These ladies believe in shopping til you drop and I carried all the packages. I'm starved."

Over his shoulder, Toby glimpsed Abby lean toward Russ and pat his arm. "But you were so helpful, Russ. I don't know what we would've done without you."

Russ blushed under such praise.

Toby was green with envy. Elizabeth wouldn't even look at him. "Did you shop a lot, too, Elizabeth?"

"Yes, I did. I bought the outfit I'm wearing tonight. Do you like it?"

Now, she'd done it. He knew she wasn't going to be pleased with his words. "You look terrific, but, well, isn't it a little sexy? I mean, there'll be a lot of

cowboys out there tonight who might think you're—
I mean, it fits you well and—men like—''

"I think I get your drift, Mr. Randall. Just pull over
and I'll find a cab and go back to the hotel!'' Elizabeth snapped, her cheeks red.

Toby kept driving, frantically trying to rephrase his
words. But he was in such a hole with Elizabeth by
that time, if he judged by her expression, that he figured that would be *Mission: Impossible*.

He looked in the rearview mirror and realized the
pair in the back seat were laughing. "What's so
funny?'' he demanded, irritation in his voice.

Abby covered her mouth with her hand and looked
away. Russ tried to stop laughing. "It's just that, well,
you're usually so good with words, Tobe, and for a
man who wanted to say the lady looked good, you
sure put your foot in it.''

With a sigh, Toby admitted, "Yeah, I did, didn't
I? Elizabeth, you're a vision and every man who sees
you is going to want to follow you home. Is that better?''

"Yes,'' she said, not looking at him, "though it
does make me feel a little like a juicy bone.''

He couldn't get it right tonight, that was for sure.
Fortunately, the restaurant was nearby. He pulled into
a parking space. His pleasant evening had gone to hell
in a handbasket.

Chapter Nine

Elizabeth hid a smile as she slid out of the truck. At least she'd accomplished her goal. Toby had noticed the change in her appearance. She'd spent time in the beauty shop this afternoon in addition to shopping. She was glad it had been worth it.

The waiter escorted them to a booth in the restaurant, and she and Abby each slid into opposite sides, facing each other, leaving the guys the outside. Elizabeth knew that would mean that Toby would be sitting beside her. Shivers coursed through her body. "You're being ridiculous!" she muttered.

"You say something?" Toby asked, leaning toward her after he was seated.

"No! This is a nice restaurant. Very...nice." Her lame compliment wasn't much, but she hoped it would distract Toby.

"I'm glad you like it. The steaks are good."

As if the food mattered. She laughed silently. Was she on a fool's errand? Toby obviously had no realization of her intent. He had no personal interest in her. She was just his cousin. She sighed.

Though Toby looked at her out of the corner of his eye, he turned to Russ and asked him a question about activities on the ranch.

And that was how the evening went. The food was good, but it didn't matter. She could scarcely eat. She and Abby occasionally discussed the decor or something at school, but Toby and Russ talked ranching, occasionally switching to the possibility of Russ working with Bill.

Her new hairstyle, her clothes, neither did anything to catch Toby's attention in a positive way.

As they left the restaurant, Abby leaned over to whisper, "Don't give up."

Elizabeth gave her a smile and resolved to hide her misery better. She didn't want everyone to know how pitiful she was.

Toby took her arm and escorted her around the truck to the passenger side, even though Russ and Abby were with them. She looked up at him, surprised.

He didn't say anything, but he continued to touch her while Russ and Abby crawled in the back seat. Then he helped her in and closed the door before rounding the truck to slide behind the wheel.

When they got to the rodeo and parked, Toby reached over and held her arm, stopping her from getting out.

"Look, Elizabeth, I know you don't like me to tell

you what to do, but this isn't home. The men here are—when they see you, they're going to want to get to know you. Don't go off with anyone. Stay close to me. Okay?''

She'd lived away from home for four years, while in college, and managed. She figured she could manage here. But it occurred to her that if she stayed next to Toby, it would keep other women from hitting on him. "Okay."

He appeared dumbfounded. "Okay?"

"Of course, Toby. Whatever you say."

He looked at the other two, then back at Elizabeth. "Is this Elizabeth Randall? Or have the gypsies stolen her and left a stranger in her place?"

"You're acting like I have no sense!" Elizabeth protested.

"Yeah," he agreed with a grin.

She couldn't help smiling back, wishing she could throw her arms around his neck and kiss him. He released her arm and she opened the truck door and slid to the ground. By that time, he'd hurried around the truck to take her arm.

"Didn't you believe me?" she asked.

"Just making sure."

Once Russ and Abby were out, Toby warned Russ. "You'd better keep hold of Abby, too. It can get pretty hectic here."

"No problem," Russ assured Toby. He was already holding Abby's hand. But he released it and wrapped an arm around her shoulders. "Okay, Abby?"

"Fine," she assured him, beaming. No one looking at them would've disagreed.

"Good idea," Toby muttered and wrapped his arm around Elizabeth, too, and she gave a silent prayer of thanks. Leaning into his warmth, she couldn't have been happier.

Toby had been right. It was crowded and they were soon surrounded by people wanting to say hello. Women.

Elizabeth put her arm around Toby's waist as woman after woman stopped them, wanting to talk to Toby, to touch him, to ask him questions.

One woman in particular pushed forward.

"Toby! I looked for you earlier to see about dinner. Where did you go?"

"Hi, Sally. My cousins came to town." Toby introduced them to Sally Tompkins, a barrel racer. "We all went to dinner."

"When are you leaving? I want a chance to talk you out of going. Can we visit after the show?" She reached out and stroked his chest.

Elizabeth wanted to slap her.

Toby cleared his throat and told her he couldn't meet her. Besides, he wasn't going to change his mind.

Elizabeth breathed a sigh of relief.

Then he drew them toward the chutes so he could

wish Lonnie good luck. Elizabeth stepped forward to pet Cocoa. The horse nickered softly in recognition.

"Hey, so you're a friend of Cocoa?" the lanky cowboy asked, his gaze traveling over her.

Elizabeth smiled. "Cocoa and I go way back."

Toby had gotten distracted by several cowboys. Lonnie looked at him and then at Elizabeth. "Don't tell me you're his cousin."

"Why, yes, I'm Elizabeth."

"Man, Toby's a lucky guy. I'm Lonnie. I'm riding Cocoa."

"Yes. Toby said you're doing very well."

"I'd have to be an idiot not to do well with this guy," he said, rubbing Cocoa's nose. "I'm going to get Toby to train a horse for me."

Elizabeth smiled and nodded.

"Hey, you want to celebrate after the show tonight? If I win, we'll have a big blowout. If I don't, we can still party. I'd like to get to know you better," Lonnie said, stepping even closer to Elizabeth.

Suddenly Toby's wide shoulders came between them. "Back off, Lonnie. We'll probably go back to the hotel after the show. Elizabeth will be tired."

Elizabeth started to protest on the general principle that she could make her own decisions, but Toby wrapped his arm around her again and introduced several other cowboys standing nearby. They offered extravagant compliments and several suggestions for what they'd like to do with her later, but Toby declined every invitation.

"Hey, Tobe, you're not giving us a chance. Back off, man. She's your cousin, not your girlfriend," one cowboy protested.

"Her daddy will hold me responsible. You don't want to mess with Chad Randall," Toby assured him.

"Not if he's kin to you," the man responded under his breath.

Elizabeth smiled. Toby was a lot more fierce and protective than her father, she thought.

"We'd better go take our seats. They're ready to start the grand parade." Toby turned her in the direction of the stands and started walking.

"What about Russ and Abby?"

"They're already there. They got tired of standing around while half the cowboys here lined up to be introduced to you."

"Don't be silly. There were only a couple. Not half as many as the women you attract."

"Those are just friends saying hello."

She stopped in her tracks. "Like Sally? Somehow I don't think she's just a 'friend.' Or at least, that's not what she *wants* to be."

Toby tugged her along, ignoring her words, but she saw the telltale blush on his cheeks. Aha!

"She and her husband recently divorced so she's— a little lost."

"But you're not ready to settle down?" She wanted to know his reaction to the idea.

"Not with her."

Well, that didn't tell her much.

They reached the front-row box seats Toby had gotten for them. Russ and Abby were sitting in the second row of seats, just behind them.

"You guys can have the front row," Toby offered with a frown.

"Naw, Abby says she's afraid a bull will jump in her lap if she sits down there," Russ said with a laugh.

Toby gestured to the chair for Elizabeth and she sat down. Then he settled beside her. When he turned around to talk to Russ, he put his arm on the back of her chair and she was once again surrounded by his warmth.

Throughout the rodeo, Toby kept his arm there, giving Elizabeth a running commentary of the action, whispering in her ear. He could've been speaking Chinese for all the attention she paid to his words. She was concentrating on his scent, his warmth, his strength.

"There's Sally," he announced, leaning forward in his chair to root his friend on. Which meant he took his arm from around her.

For that reason alone, Elizabeth wasn't fond of Sally. Knowing the woman was free and interested in Toby really didn't endear her to Elizabeth, but she clapped politely for Sally's magnificent run. She didn't mind if Sally won the barrel racing, as long as she didn't win Toby.

Since his arm came around her again, Elizabeth

relaxed and even smiled when Toby commented on how well Sally had done.

"Has she been barrel racing long?" she asked.

"Ten years. She started when she was seventeen. It's a hard life."

"Yes, it must be." Elizabeth felt sympathy for the other woman. She was grateful for the home she had and the family support.

He squeezed her shoulder. "You're lucky."

"So are you, but you came to the rodeo anyway. Why?"

He looked away. "I guess the excitement."

"But now you don't need the excitement anymore?" She'd wondered about both his decisions, the one sending him to the rodeo and the one bringing him home.

"I don't know."

Her heart clutched at the hint that he might return to the rodeo. "What do you mean? Surely you wouldn't—"

He didn't look at her. Or answer her question. "We'll see." He pointed out that Lonnie was up next. As if Lonnie mattered in the scheme of things.

Lonnie won the steer-wrestling and calf-roping events. When the evening ended, several cowboys came up to talk to Toby about his training a horse for Lonnie. Elizabeth praised Toby's training methods. She'd rather have him on the ranch, training horses, than in the rodeo. At least on the ranch all these women wouldn't be around.

Lonnie was excited about his wins and wanted them to join him in a celebration. Elizabeth looked at Abby, but her friend, standing arm in arm with Russ, answered her unspoken question with a negative nod.

"Thank you, Lonnie," Elizabeth responded, "but I'm afraid we're making an early start in the morning. We'd better go back to the hotel, but thank you for asking us."

Several cowboys standing around argued with them, but Toby wasn't one of them. Elizabeth decided he must be tired of escorting cousins and want to be on his own. Especially when he half promised to meet the others later.

"We can make our own way to the hotel, Toby, if you want to party with your friends," she said stiffly as he led them back to his truck.

He frowned and slowed his pace. "What are you talking about?"

"You said—"

"I was just being polite. I don't want to join them and they don't care. They only wanted you to join them." Then he took hold of her arm and pulled her toward the truck, as if they were in a hurry.

"They don't know me!" she protested.

"No, but they want to. I told you how it would be with you dressing so sexy. They couldn't keep their eyes off you." He pulled out his keys and unlocked the truck door.

When they were all settled in the truck, Russ leaned forward. "You want to swing by your motel room and check out? You could spend the night with me at the hotel.''

''Thanks, but we'd have to come back here to load up Cocoa. I'll just stay where I am. What time are you willing to start in the morning?''

''Seven?'' Russ offered and Abby groaned.

''Too early for you, sweetheart?'' Russ hurriedly asked. ''Maybe we could make it eight. I'll tell you what, Toby, we'll take a cab out here at eight. Then you won't have to drive into downtown pulling the trailer. Would that make up for the late start?''

''I can get up,'' Abby protested. ''I didn't mean— It's just that sleeping in sounded good.''

''It's only four or five hours home,'' Toby said. ''Sure we can wait to get started.'' He stared at Elizabeth.

She shrugged. ''Eight o'clock works for me. We can eat an early lunch in Casper and then drive on home. It will break up the trip.'' She figured Abby would go with Russ when they picked up his truck, leaving her a couple of hours with Toby and no one else.

''Okay. Don't eat breakfast until you meet me. I know a great place and I'll treat.'' Toby grinned at them. ''They even have better pancakes than Red's, but don't tell him I said so.''

TOBY WATCHED the threesome go into the hotel. He knew what Russ was counting on. A goodnight kiss. He wished he'd had any hope of that from Elizabeth.

After cradling her against him all evening, his motor was revved.

But Elizabeth wouldn't even have considered offering him the kind of kiss he wanted. He was her cousin. And tonight, he'd been testing himself, trying to determine if he was going to be able to live on the ranch with her, and still keep his passion for her a secret.

Maybe. As long as he didn't test himself too much…or expect too much. Maybe he'd find someone he could enjoy. Build a future.

He played with that thought a little while as he drove back to the rodeo. Then he dismissed it. He couldn't think of a future with another woman. At least not now.

But he could be with his family. That would have to be enough.

With that weighty decision made, he returned to the room he'd rented all week, carefully avoiding the cowboys who were milling around, celebrating the end of another week of rodeo. That life was no longer for him.

His day started early the next morning as he packed and then tended to Cocoa. To his surprise, Lonnie dragged himself from his bed to remind Toby again that he'd agreed to train a horse for him…at a hefty price.

"Sure you don't want to give me a bargain?"

Toby grinned at his old friend. "One of my horses would be a bargain at any price."

"True. Sure you don't want to loan me Cocoa the rest of the way?"

"Nope, I can't do that. I'd miss him too much."

"Okay, okay," Lonnie agreed, but he stood there watching Toby, not leaving.

"When are you packing up?" Toby asked, a subtle hint.

"In a little while. Your cousins goin' back with you?"

"Yeah," Toby said. "We're going to breakfast and then hitting the road."

"Hey, breakfast sounds good! I'll join you," Lonnie announced with a big smile. "You don't mind, do you?"

Now Toby knew why Lonnie got up early. "Does it matter if I do?"

"Nope. Your cousin is a looker."

"Back off, friend."

"Hey! I'm a good guy," Lonnie protested.

"Look, Lonnie, she's—"

"Good morning!" Elizabeth called out as she approached them. She was dressed in jeans and a green sweater, her magnificent hair pulled back in a long curling ponytail.

Toby thought she looked more like the Elizabeth he'd always known, but she was still beautiful.

"Good morning, gorgeous," Lonnie immediately responded, stepping forward to take her hand.

Toby immediately inserted himself between the two and clasped Elizabeth's shoulders to place a kiss or her forehead. "Morning, cuz. Everyone feeling okay this morning?"

Russ was loaded down with all their packages from their shopping expedition the day before and their overnight bags. "Point me to the truck so I can unload," he ordered. "Then I'll be all right."

"We offered to help him," Abby said, her attention focused on Russ. "But he refused."

Toby was torn between offering to help Russ and leaving Lonnie alone with Elizabeth. Finally he found a solution. "Lonnie, while I find my keys, will you help Russ with the packages and bags?"

Elizabeth stepped over to pat Cocoa as Lonnie reluctantly took some of Russ's load. Toby then pulled his keys out of his jean pockets. "Oh, here are the keys. Come on, guys, I'm just parked right over here."

Lonnie gave Toby a suspicious look, but he followed him and his cousin. When they returned, Lonnie announced that he was joining them at breakfast if Elizabeth—after a pause, he quickly added Abby— didn't mind.

Much to Toby's disgust, the ladies welcomed him warmly. Of course, without being rude, they didn't have much choice, but they didn't have to be so enthusiastic.

But Lonnie's next idea had him boiling.

"Elizabeth, why don't you ride with me to the restaurant? I'll be lonely going by myself." Lonnie smiled the way he always did to charm the ladies. He was a real social butterfly.

"No!" Toby exclaimed and then had to come up with an excuse. "Uh, take Russ with you. He takes up the most room."

Lonnie sent him a knowing look. "A-huh."

"Sure, I'll ride with you, Lonnie," Russ agreed after receiving a stare from Toby. But he sent a lingering look at Abby.

Toby urged the two women toward his truck. Russ could do without Abby's company for the five minutes it would take to get to the restaurant.

Elizabeth slid into the truck first, putting her next to Toby. Abby asked something about Elizabeth getting carsick, and Toby stared at her. He'd never known Elizabeth to have a sensitive stomach. "Carsick?"

Elizabeth grinned. "No, I don't get carsick, but I used that excuse to make sure Abby sat beside Russ. I was matchmaking."

Abby looked shocked and Elizabeth laughed. "You didn't mind, did you?"

The smile that covered Abby's face made her look beautiful. "Oh, no. I didn't mind. This weekend has been the best time of my life."

Elizabeth leaned over and hugged her and Toby felt like he should, too. "We're happy for you, Abby," he said gently. "Russ is a lucky guy."

Abby's cheeks burned bright red. "Oh, he hasn't...I mean, we're just—I had a good time."

Toby pulled into the parking lot of the restaurant. "Good. That's the idea. Let's go eat. I'm starving."

Russ and Lonnie had got there before them and already had a table. Both men were standing at the table, waiting to seat the ladies.

It didn't take Toby long to figure out that Lonnie wanted Elizabeth all to himself. It took some maneuvering to manage to snag the seat on the other side of her. There was no way to block Lonnie out completely.

The waitress was waiting for them to be seated, ready to take the orders. When that business was taken care of, Lonnie immediately claimed Elizabeth's attention, asking personal questions about her. Toby leaned forward and answered one of his questions.

"Hey! I was asking Elizabeth."

"He can probably answer most of your questions, Lonnie," Elizabeth said, much to Toby's delight. "He knows me well."

That last statement made him pause. He hadn't been around her in about seven years. How well did he know her?

Once the food was delivered, conversation became general and light. They were all hungry.

It also meant the breakfast was ending, and Toby would no longer have to worry about Lonnie preying on Elizabeth. He began to relax, eager to hit the road with Elizabeth beside him.

"You know what," Lonnie began, putting down his fork. "I just had a great idea."

Toby tensed. This wasn't good.

"If your folks have a spare bed, Tobe, I think I'll go back to Wyoming with you so I can pick out the horse you're going to train for me."

All the others looked at Toby. He swallowed, trying not to choke on his food. What could he say?

"That's not necessary, Lonnie. You know you can trust me."

"I know, pal, but I need a break. The rodeo next week isn't a big one. I can afford to miss it. And besides," he added, a big grin on his face. "I'll get to spend more time with Elizabeth."

Chapter Ten

Elizabeth wasn't sure what was going on, but Toby seemed agitated. She didn't think he wanted Lonnie to come home with them.

"I'm sure our parents would welcome you, Lonnie, but you won't see much of me. I teach kindergarten all day." She smiled at him; but she wasn't being rude, just truthful.

"But maybe I could see you in the evenings, even take you to a movie," Lonnie suggested, a hopeful expression on his face.

"Maybe Russ and I could go with you," Abby suggested, surprising Elizabeth. She looked at her friend and realized Abby was trying to tell her something. A subtle nod toward Toby had Elizabeth shifting her gaze to him. Could he be jealous? Was that what Abby was trying to tell her?

Toby said, "You'll be too tired to go out, pal. I'm going to work you hard."

"Hey, I thought it was the horse you were going to train," Lonnie protested, looking unhappy.

"You've got to work together. Come if you want to, but it won't be any party."

The two men stared at each other, almost as if it was a contest of some kind. The waitress returned to fill up the coffee cups and ended the duel.

"I'd like a cup to go, please," Lonnie asked.

"Late night last night?"

Lonnie looked back at Toby. "You know I'm not a morning person. A little extra caffeine won't hurt. Have you got time to wait for me to load up?"

"You're still coming?" Toby asked.

Lonnie nodded to his friend but directed his words to Elizabeth. "I wouldn't miss a chance to spend even five minutes with you, Elizabeth."

Elizabeth suddenly felt uncomfortable. She hadn't meant to give Lonnie the wrong idea when she welcomed him to breakfast. But it appeared he'd read more into her warmth than she'd meant. She felt guilty.

The glare in Toby's eyes told her he thought she was guilty, too.

"There really won't be that much time, Lonnie," she warned him.

"I'm comin'," he replied with determination.

"Well, we're not waiting around for a couple of hours. I told the family we'd be home pretty early and I've got some things I need to do."

"Fine. I'll be there by nightfall."

The two men sounded like deadly enemies, not friends.

"Elizabeth, I'd surely like some company on the drive. Why don't you wait and ride with me?" Lonnie suggested, a warm smile on his face.

"No!" Toby exclaimed. This time he didn't even offer Elizabeth a chance to agree or disagree. "I promised her daddy I'd take care of her. You drive like a bat out of hell. She'll be riding with me."

All the friendly atmosphere disappeared completely.

"Hell, how am I going to find the place?" Lonnie growled.

Russ cleared his throat and Elizabeth saw one of his hands steal over to Abby. "I guess I could wait and ride with you if you need a guide."

Abby gasped, and Elizabeth immediately stopped that idea. She wasn't going to ruin her friend's trip. "I can draw you a good map, Lonnie. It's not hard to find. But Russ has to pick up his truck, and he promised to—to run an errand for Abby." She took a napkin and flipped it over. On the back she drew a careful map.

"And if you get lost, just give us a call," she finished with a smile and handed the map to Lonnie.

"Thanks, sweetie pie," Lonnie said, beaming at her.

"Her name's Elizabeth." Toby growled.

Lonnie shot him a cold look. He stood, announcing that he was going to start packing so he wouldn't be too far behind them.

Everyone was ready to go and they all stood. Lonnie leaned over and hugged Elizabeth, giving her a kiss on the cheek. Then he was out of the restaurant before anyone could protest.

Elizabeth avoided Toby's stare. "Are we ready to go? I think I'll visit the rest room before we leave. Abby, you want to go with me?"

As soon as they were away from the two men, Abby said, "Thanks for stopping Russ from sacrificing."

Elizabeth grinned. "I didn't see any reason for you to have your trip ruined."

"But how do you feel about all this?"

"I'm worried I might have encouraged Lonnie, but I didn't intend to."

"Of course you didn't. Though you might be able to use him," Abby added, speculation in her voice.

"What do you mean?"

"Russ has noticed Toby's behavior this weekend. He said it was like he was jealous of the other men. Bless his heart, he seems a little puzzled by it," Abby added with a chuckle. "But I think Toby is jealous as hell. And Lonnie will keep him feeling that way."

"But I can't lead Lonnie on," Elizabeth protested.

"I don't think you'll have to. It's just an idea."

Elizabeth thought about Abby's words long after they were in the truck. Toby didn't speak until they reached the rodeo grounds. In terse words, he ordered her and Abby to stay in the truck while he and Russ hooked up the trailer and got Cocoa in it.

In the silence after the men got out, Elizabeth finally said, "Well, it's going to be a pleasant ride back, isn't it?"

"I'm sure he'll relax in a while. Nobody can remain that angry forever. Besides, it's Lonnie he's mad at, not you."

"I wouldn't take any bets on that," Elizabeth muttered.

BY THE TIME they stopped for lunch in Casper before Russ picked up his truck, Elizabeth didn't care who Toby was mad at. She was tired of his childish behavior.

She stopped Toby as Russ and Abby went into the restaurant.

"Toby Randall, you need to stop being childish. It's not our fault that your friend decided to follow you home. You're making us all miserable with your sulking!"

Toby looked at Elizabeth as if she were a space alien.

"You've got to be kidding! Not your fault? Who do you think he's coming to see? Not me, Elizabeth."

"But all I did was act friendly to a friend of yours. Nothing else. I didn't invite him!"

"You sure didn't discourage him!"

"I tried! I told him I'd be busy."

"Yeah, you did. Okay, okay, it's not your fault. Except that you're so damn pretty."

Elizabeth kept her grin in check. "I wish I thought that was a compliment."

That broke through his anger. "You know it is, brat. Come on, let's go get some lunch. Being angry makes me hungry."

"Then I hope you've got lots of money because your appetite must be as big as the Rocky Mountains today."

He pushed her ahead of him, then lightly swatted her on her bottom. "Behave yourself!"

Over her shoulder, she assured him with a grin, "I always do."

Once they were seated at the table, Russ said, "You feeling better, Toby?"

"Yeah, I apologize. I let some things bother me, but it wasn't your fault. I should've behaved better. Hope I didn't ruin your trip," he said, smiling at the other two.

Abby shook her head and smiled.

Russ said, "Nope. That would only have happened if I'd had to ride with Lonnie."

"I appreciated your offer, Russ. But he really does drive like a maniac. I didn't want any of us riding with him." He picked up the menu and changed the subject to food.

Elizabeth was pleased. The old Toby was back. He wasn't mad at her anymore. Now she could look forward to the two-hour drive home. Just her and Toby.

Maybe she'd made a little progress after all. He'd told her she was pretty.

Most of the drive from Casper, just the two of them in the truck, was pleasant. Toby asked her to tell him about teaching, wanting to know if she enjoyed it. Once she started talking about her babies, she forgot the passage of time.

"Sounds like it's going to be hard on you when the school year ends," he said. "You're not going to want to let them go."

"It will be hard, but I'll see them again. They'll be in Abby's class next year, or the other first-grade teacher's room. And they're just across the hall."

"So, do you want babies of your own?"

"Of course I do! Several. Mom and Dad would never forgive me if I didn't provide more babies. You know how the Randalls are about babies." She grinned at him. The family history was a well-known tale.

Toby smiled in return. "Yeah. I was there when the twins were born. And then the others, including you. Makes the place seem calm now, with all of us, or most of us, grown up."

"Poor Casey, always the baby."

"Yeah, but once the next generation starts coming along, he'll be Uncle Casey. That'll make him feel grown-up."

Elizabeth sighed. "But it may be a while before that next generation appears. You're the oldest and you don't seem interested in having babies." Then she brightened. "Maybe Russ and Abby will—I think he's interested, don't you?"

"I don't know if he's interested in babies, but you

can safely say he's interested in Abby," Toby agreed. "He kept his hands on her all weekend."

"That doesn't mean anything. You kept yours on me, like I was an escaped prisoner or something," she pointed out.

"I was trying to keep you safe. I told you that." He kept his eyes on the road but she saw his hands tighten on the wheel.

"Well, I'm glad we're going to be back home so you won't have to worry about me!" she snapped, irritated by his attitude. And their ride had been so pleasant until now.

"I want to warn you now. Don't go off with Lonnie, even on a simple errand. He's not to be trusted."

"If he's that awful, why is he your friend?"

"It's just with women that he—he's fine when it comes to horses and…things."

"That doesn't make sense at all. He's either a good person or he isn't. You can't divide life up like that."

"It's a man thing, Elizabeth. Just do what I say. And don't for any reason get in a vehicle with him."

"Toby, I'm an adult. We've been through this before. I can make my own decisions," she returned, folding her arms over her chest.

"Yeah, but I might not be around to save you next time."

His drawl made her feel weak and stupid. "I am not an idiot. I'll manage."

"Do what I say!" he snapped back.

She stared straight ahead, ignoring him. Fortunately, they'd reached the ranch road leading to the house. Maybe they'd be home before they actually got in a fight.

"Elizabeth?"

She didn't acknowledge his one word in any way. His voice may have changed to all sweetness, but she knew he was trying to coax her to agree to his rules.

"Elizabeth, I just want to keep you safe. Please?"

"You're not sweet-talking me into putting you in charge of my life, Toby. You can't disappear for so long and then think you can tell me what to do. I've grown up."

"That's the problem," he muttered.

A sound distracted him and he looked in his rear-view mirror. "Damn!"

"What is it?" she asked, looking over her shoulder to see a pickup coming up fast behind them.

"It's Lonnie. I told you he was a crazy driver."

"He must not have stopped for lunch," Elizabeth speculated.

"His mind wasn't on food. I hope Mom and Dad don't mind him staying a week. I should've called them."

"You know they won't mind. They're always inviting people to stay. Besides, they want you to stay here and train horses, not return to the rodeo. They'll do anything to encourage you."

ON FRIDAY, Toby leaned against the corral and watched Lonnie put the horse they'd ultimately cho-

sen through its paces. It had taken them longer than
Toby had expected to select the right horse. Like him,
Lonnie was tall, but he didn't have the bulk Toby had.
The best horse was a little too strong for Lonnie to
control.

That delay had been time-consuming. Not a bad
thing. It had ensured Lonnie not having much time
for Elizabeth. And, much to Toby's approval, she
hadn't encouraged his friend.

But the weekend was here. Elizabeth wouldn't be
in school. And Lonnie had already talked about taking
her into town tonight.

He figured that meant he'd have to waste his Friday
night in town, too, sticking to Lonnie and Elizabeth
like glue.

He saw the men riding in. Russ had spent the first
half of the week in town with Bill, having lunch with
Abby each day. But tonight he was here on the ranch.
Toby wondered if he'd made plans with Abby.

Waving Lonnie to a halt, he indicated they should
take care of the horse and go to dinner. In the barn,
joining the other men, he pulled Russ aside.

"You got plans with Abby tonight?"

Russ grinned. "Yeah. Our first real date."

"Ah. Congratulations. I guess you don't want company, do you?"

"Uh, well, we could—"

"Never mind. I'm not going to make you suffer.
Enjoy yourself. Are you going to the movies?"

"Yeah, after dinner. I'm taking her to that fancy steak place in Buffalo."

"Sounds like a good plan," Toby assured him, all the while trying to figure out how he was going to keep Elizabeth out of his friend's clutches.

Rich stepped over to his twin's side. "What are we going to do tonight?"

Russ ducked his head. "I've got a date."

Rich didn't appear happy. "You didn't tell me."

"I forgot. Abby and I planned it a couple of days ago and...I forgot to mention it." He slapped his horse on its flank as a goodbye and slid away from his twin.

"Maybe I can find a date and we can double," Rich called as Russ moved away.

Russ turned and nodded. "Sure, uh, that would be fine. We're going to dinner as soon as I can get cleaned up, so hurry." Then he rushed away.

Toby had kind of envied the twins when they were younger. They always had each other, no matter who else was involved in whatever they were doing. Now he could see it might be a problem. "Hey, Rich, I think Russ and Abby want to be alone."

"I know," Rich said, his teeth gritted.

"You have something against Abby?"

"Yeah. She wants to marry my brother!"

"It's gonna happen someday, Rich. At least Abby's a nice girl, and she's crazy about Russ."

With a sigh, Rich agreed. "I'll adjust. It's just—strange."

"How about you hang out with me and Lonnie tonight?"

Toby shifted his gaze to his friend. "Lonnie, are we hitting the town tonight?"

Lonnie didn't look at him. "I need to talk to Elizabeth first. See what she wants to do."

"I imagine she'll want to stay in and rest," Toby said, knowing that wasn't what Lonnie would want to hear.

"Give it up, Toby. You've kept me away from her all week. It's Friday night. Let Elizabeth speak for herself."

"We'll see." Toby turned around, ready to head for the house and get a word with Elizabeth before Lonnie could talk to her. If she was going into town, he'd be going with her, Lonnie or no Lonnie.

Rich stared at the two men. "This could be interesting," he muttered and hurried after Toby.

Lonnie was right behind them.

ELIZABETH was tired. The children had been restless. The excitement of school starting had worn off. The realization that school wasn't all fun and games had set in. It took a lot more effort to keep the kids happy.

Plus, the tension at home was wearing. Every evening, Lonnie had wanted to spend time with her. It took a lot of effort to entertain a stranger, especially when he wanted so much more than she had any interest in giving.

Then there was Toby. He'd followed her around

like a pet Rottweiler, threatening to snap off any of Lonnie's body parts that got close to her.

Keeping the peace between Toby and his friend took even more effort. She'd had enough. And had taken her own action to end it.

With a determined smile on her face, she climbed the stairs, planning a soothing bubble bath to start her evening.

A knock on the bathroom door shocked her as she relaxed in the hot bubbly water. "Yes?"

"Elizabeth?"

With a sigh, she asked, "What do you want, Toby?"

"Lonnie's downstairs wanting to ask you what you want to do tonight. You do remember all the things I warned you about?"

She swirled the bubbles in the water, a smile on her lips. "How could I forget? You've been reminding me every day. Now go away."

"Elizabeth, I think it would be good if we planned what to do this evening. You know, if you say you want us all to go into town together, then I could drive, and I could help you keep Lonnie at a distance."

"Really?" she asked, her voice heavy with sarcasm.

"Elizabeth!"

"Go away, Toby. I'm trying to relax. Today was difficult. I'll be downstairs in about half an hour."

The door rattled, giving Elizabeth a shock. "Don't open that door!" she squealed.

"I'm not, but I think you're being difficult!"

"Go away!"

To her surprise, he did.

The water was getting cold, but now she had to stay in the tub another few minutes on principle if nothing else. She certainly didn't want Toby thinking he had intimidated her. She was determined to make her own choices.

She timed her arrival downstairs for exactly half an hour later. Dinner was over and everyone was sitting around talking. She'd had several discussions with her mother during the week about Toby's attitude. Her mother had encouraged her to trust her own judgment.

When she entered, Toby and Lonnie leaped to their feet and came around the table to greet her.

Elizabeth slipped around them to go to her father. "Hi, Daddy. It's been a busy week, and I've scarcely seen you."

"I know, baby. You're looking good tonight."

"Thank you," she said, and bent to kiss his cheek.

"You going out?" her father asked.

"Yes, I am," she assured him, again ignoring anyone else's reaction.

"Want any company?" Rich asked.

"Hey, you can't—" Lonnie protested. Then he collected himself. "I was going to ask the same thing, Elizabeth. You can hang out with Rich whenever, but

I have to leave tomorrow. How about going out with me?''

''I think we should all go out together,'' Toby argued, staring at Lonnie. ''There isn't a lot to do here, so we might as well all enjoy ourselves.''

''Next thing I know you'll be inviting her parents, too!'' Lonnie roared. Then turned bright red. ''I mean—I didn't mean any disrespect, Mr. Randall. But I'd like to spend some time with Elizabeth without half her family hanging around.''

''How nice of you, Lonnie. Too bad you didn't say something before now,'' Elizabeth said with a smile. Then she stepped over to the hooks on the wall where they all hung their jackets. Taking hers down, she turned to look at the three handsome men standing there, ready to escort her wherever.

''I already have plans for tonight.'' Then she walked out the door.

Chapter Eleven

Toby figured he'd never understand women. Elizabeth *knew* Lonnie wanted her to go out with him.

Then he had to move because Lonnie was already out the door following Elizabeth. Rich came after him.

"Elizabeth, wait!" Lonnie called.

Toby caught up with him just as he reached Elizabeth.

"Yes?" she asked as she pulled car keys from her purse.

"Where are you going? You knew I wanted to see you," Lonnie pointed out.

Toby decided his friend wasn't as fast a learner as him. He wouldn't have pointed that out, since it appeared to be a factor in her behavior.

As if explaining the rules of life to a child, Elizabeth said, "Lonnie, a gentleman extends an invitation ahead of time when he wants to see a lady. And not at the last minute."

Which left Lonnie red-cheeked and tongue-tied.

"Where you going, Lizzie?" Rich asked.

"The church hayride. Didn't you hear about it?"

"Oh, yeah. I forgot. Mind if I go with you?"

"No, I don't mind. Even better, I'm sure the others won't mind either. It will cost you five dollars, of course, and you'd better go call and tell them you're coming or they won't have enough hot dogs."

A hayride. Toby decided that might be better than heading to the bar in town. There'd be less single guys at the hayride. All the women would have drafted them as dates.

"Mind if we come, too?" Toby asked casually.

When she shook her head, he asked Rich to add their names to the list.

While Rich was inside, Lonnie tried to apologize his way out of the hole he was in. "Uh, Elizabeth, I'm sorry. I wasn't thinking. I mean, I was thinking of you, but I forgot the social niceties. It's Toby's fault. He—he distracted me. I intended to—"

"Lonnie, don't worry about it. I'm sure you'll enjoy the hayride. We'll cook hot dogs and visit. And they're nice people."

Toby couldn't resist teasing his friend. "Yeah, but mind your mouth. They don't approve of cursing."

"Hey! I don't— I mean, on occasion, but I wouldn't— I'll be careful."

Elizabeth sent an admonishing glance at Toby, but she said nothing.

Rich came out the back door and sprang off the porch. "All set. Mrs. Smith said she had extra hot dogs and as long as we paid her five dollars, we were welcome.''

They finally agreed to take the Jeep Elizabeth drove. Toby offered to drive, but Elizabeth pointed out that it was her car. She slid behind the wheel and the other three jumped for the empty seats before she left without them.

''I wonder why Russ didn't take Abby to this,'' Rich muttered. ''It would've been a lot cheaper.''

Elizabeth sighed. ''Because you don't impress a girl by being cheaper, and I don't think he wanted to share her company with every cowboy in the county.''

''She's got a point there,'' Toby agreed.

''Do you think he's serious?'' Rich asked.

''She's pretty enough,'' Lonnie pointed out and was surprised when Elizabeth glared at him over her shoulder.

''There's a lot more to Abby than being pretty!''

''Well, yeah, but—of course,'' Lonnie agreed, cutting short any attempt to justify his words.

Toby, having captured the front seat next to Elizabeth, decided keeping silent might be his best choice. Not that he disagreed with her. Elizabeth was beautiful, but he'd been with other beautiful women. It wasn't her beauty alone that had captured his heart long ago.

Once they reached the meeting point for the hayride, he introduced Lonnie to Mrs. Smith, one of his teachers from long ago.

"I'm glad you decided to come. We have several others who didn't come with dates, so you'll have people to talk to," she said briskly and pointed them to the wagon.

It suddenly occurred to Toby that Elizabeth might have arranged to meet someone here. He hurried over to the wagon, Lonnie trailing after him.

"Elizabeth?" he called.

From the sound of her voice as she responded, he guessed she was on the other side of the pile of hay. He hurried around to find her sitting with a group of young people.

"Mind if we join you?" he said to the group in general. He was relieved to see there were more females than hungry males in the group.

Before he and Lonnie could get settled, the wagon started to roll. "Rich? Did you make it on?" he called out.

His cousin waved from the front of the wagon. It appeared he'd already found a young lady to snuggle up to.

A half hour later, Toby had discovered several truths. Neither he nor Lonnie were going to get close to Elizabeth any time soon. And they should've brought a blanket.

The hay was scratchy and the wind was cold.

When they reached the place for dinner, the driver pulled the horses to a halt and jumped off to bring a short stepladder to the side so everyone could get down.

Toby jumped down, ignoring the lineup. Then he moved over to the ladder to offer his assistance. Which meant he put his hands around Elizabeth's small waist and swung her to the ground, ignoring the rest of the ladder.

Unfortunately, it also meant he couldn't follow her. He still had a line of ladies wanting assistance. Damn!

Lonnie immediately strode alongside Elizabeth, murmuring in her ear.

Mrs. Smith began organizing her troops to prepare the hot dogs. She recruited wood gatherers. Since Elizabeth volunteered to gather wood, Lonnie and Toby did, too.

"Over there, Toby," Lonnie called. "There's some good wood."

Toby, however, knew his friend's tricks. "Yeah. Come on, Elizabeth." He took her hand and tugged her in that direction.

"No! I mean— There's some smaller pieces over here for Elizabeth." Lonnie pointed in the opposite direction.

"You get those, Lonnie," Toby said. "Elizabeth and I will get these."

Elizabeth muffled her chuckle so only Toby could hear it. "I think you're frustrating your friend."

"Damn right. He had no intention of gathering wood."

"But you're so hungry you're keeping us on the right track?"

"Yeah, right. Hunger. That's what's driving me."

Since he was wearing gloves, he insisted on picking up the wood initially to be sure there were no creepy-crawlies. Then he handed a few sticks to Elizabeth. "That's enough. Let's go back and start cooking."

They beat Lonnie back to the fire. When he finally arrived with his load of firewood, Toby and Elizabeth were seated on the ground, leaning against a tree, eating their hot dogs.

He filled his plate and joined them, but he wasn't a happy camper.

"I brought back more wood," Lonnie said, glaring at Toby.

"You certainly did, Lonnie. Good job," Elizabeth said soothingly.

A female voice interrupted them. "Do you mind if I join you?"

A young woman whom Elizabeth vaguely knew had apparently decided Elizabeth had more than her share of men. She seemed pleasant, though very determined. Elizabeth greeted her with a nod and a smile. Lonnie, after a bitter look at Toby, turned his attention to the young lady. They wandered off a few minutes later, hand in hand.

Toby carefully noted that Elizabeth didn't show any distress over Lonnie's abandonment of her. "You okay with that?"

"What?"

"Lonnie finding another girl."

Elizabeth chuckled. "I'm pretty sure his infatuation

with me had a lot to do with your pushing him away.''

"Don't be silly,'' Toby told her.

"Anyway, she's much more interested in him than I am.'' She jumped to her feet. "Come on, let's go find us a good seat before everyone else is finished.''

That suited Toby. He would help Elizabeth on and then follow her. He didn't want to be stuck with helping all the other women. Before he'd be able to get to her side, she'd be surrounded by the other men.

The rest of the evening, they leaned against each other in the hay and talked to their neighbors. Toby couldn't remember when he'd spent a better evening.

The last half hour of the evening, however, a cold front blew through. The wind picked up, and its sting grew colder. Toby pulled Elizabeth against him, wrapped her inside his coat and huddled with her until the ride ended. Though they were still cold, Toby felt warmth inside him. He would've gladly taken another half hour with Elizabeth pressed tightly against him.

They ran for the car as soon as their feet hit the ground. This time Toby took the wheel and Elizabeth didn't protest. He warmed up the engine while they waited for Lonnie and Rich to say good-night to the women they'd found.

"Man, that heater feels good,'' Rich said as they slammed the doors behind them. "I didn't know a norther was on the way.''

Toby said, "I heard Uncle Pete say something

about one tomorrow. I guess it got here faster than expected."

"I'm glad I'm heading south in the morning. I'm going to Reno for the big rodeo," Lonnie said.

"You won't be much warmer there," Toby warned him.

"Warm enough. It's in the valley. I'll be gone by the time you get up, Elizabeth."

There was an awkward silence, as if he expected Elizabeth to plead with him not to go.

She smiled over her shoulder and said, "I hope you have a safe trip, Lonnie. And I hope you win. We'll be watching for the results."

"I'd have a better chance if I could take Cocoa with me."

"Your regular ride will have recovered from the sprain, Lonnie. You know that," Toby reminded him.

"Yeah, but Cocoa is better."

"I know, but I'm training Buster. He'll be ready next year." Toby wasn't going to send Cocoa off with Lonnie. He tended to be careless with his livestock. It was all right as long as Toby was there, but he wouldn't betray Cocoa's trust by loaning him to Lonnie without him there to care for him.

"Some of the other guys were talking about getting you to train for them, too. I hope you don't." Lonnie added, "Promise me?"

"Can't do that, Lonnie," Toby said. "I'm thinking about starting up a business. I'll train horses and maybe even train riders. Make a little extra cash."

"Like you need it. Being in all those ads must pay a pretty penny."

"Yeah, but if you win this season, you'll begin getting some offers."

"You giving it up?"

"Not necessarily. I'll listen if someone calls, but it's not my favorite thing to do."

Rich laughed. "Yeah, right. Getting cozy with those glamorous models must be real tough."

Toby stole a sidelong look at Elizabeth, wondering how she was taking the conversation, but her face was turned toward the window. "It's harder than you think," he finally said.

He pulled to a halt by the house. Elizabeth was out first, and she didn't stop until she reached the porch. Then she turned suddenly, leaned toward Lonnie and kissed his cheek before he knew what she was doing. She then wished him a safe trip. By the time he caught his breath and tried to say something, she had disappeared into the house.

Lonnie stood there holding his cheek. "I guess she's not going to miss me," he said with a sad face.

Rich slapped him on the shoulder. "We've all enjoyed your visit, Lonnie."

Toby knew that wasn't what Lonnie wanted, but it was a nice gesture on Rich's part.

"I'll let you know how Buster's training goes. You just keep winning. Come on, let's hit the sack. I'll even get up early with you in the morning."

Because he was going to be glad to see the last of Lonnie.

TOBY HAD been sure Lonnie's going would be a good thing. He wouldn't have to protect Elizabeth from Lonnie's lecherous ways. He could turn his attention to work. He could concentrate on important things, like training Buster.

It was good work. He enjoyed it. But after three or four days of it, he realized it didn't satisfy him. And he had absolutely no connection with Elizabeth. No excuse to grab the seat next to her. No reason to guard her at night. No need to touch her.

Well, that wasn't true. He had a need. He remembered the last half hour of the hayride with pleasure and warmth. And need. To hold her against him, sharing a good time, almost as one.

What was he going to do?

That question popped into his mind while he was riding on Thursday and caused him to miss a calf he was trying to rope. He took a lot of razzing from his family about missing. It even wounded his pride, but he knew the reason. It wasn't that his skills were going bad. No, it was that his mind wasn't clear.

He gathered his rope and roped the calf clean as a whistle, silencing the teasing. But the question wasn't as easily silenced. What was he going to do? He couldn't live in a constant state of near-arousal, his mind elsewhere. Cowboying carried heavy consequences if you did it haphazardly.

"You all right, son?" Jake asked a few minutes later as they met at the campfire someone had built to heat the irons. They were branding the late calves that had missed the spring roundup.

"Yeah, I'm fine."

"Something on your mind?"

Toby stared at Jake. It was scary how often in his youth his father had read his mind. It seemed he still had that ability. "Yeah."

"If you want to talk, you know where I am." Jake didn't wait for an answer but mounted and started working again.

Toby grinned. Yeah, he'd always known where Jake was. And that he'd listen. What a gift the man had given Toby. A father who cared and would always listen.

But the whole point of avoiding Elizabeth for the past seven years, of promising himself he'd leave her alone, had been to keep his passions a secret from Jake. Hadn't it?

The emptiness in his head scared him. Had it been something else? He'd thought he hadn't wanted to shame Jake, and he didn't. But was there something else?

He couldn't find an answer, and Uncle Chad yelled for him to come help, so he swung up on Cocoa's back and shoved all those questions to the back of his mind. He had work to do now.

At dinner that night, he kept an eye on Elizabeth. Not to protect her but to judge his own reaction to her. Maybe he'd imagined this whole attraction thing. Maybe... No, it was still there. He still wanted to be by her side. To talk to her, to touch her, to hold her forever. Damn, that was definitely real.

He'd never even kissed her! Maybe she'd be a lousy kisser. Would he still want her? Oh, yeah. He could teach her. Maybe—

"Boy, you gonna eat my mashed potatoes or sleep?" Red yelled at him.

Toby snapped his head up to discover most of the people at the table, his family, staring at him. "Uh, sorry. I guess the week off made me soft." Then he took a bite of the offending potatoes and chewed determinedly.

When he got up to help clear the table, B.J. put a hand on his shoulder. "You don't have to help if you don't feel well, son."

"It's not that, Mom. I can help. I just have some thinking to do."

He didn't get any thinking done during the clean up because Elizabeth was helping tonight. Since she was the only female of the second generation at home, she organized her male cousins. Toby ended up beside her at the sink, rinsing the dishes she'd just washed. Their hands frequently touched, making him want more.

"Don't drop it, Toby!" she warned him as she passed him a platter. He'd been trying to avoid her touch to reduce his frustration level.

He firmly grabbed the platter. "I won't."

"Are you missing Lonnie? I thought you'd have plenty of guys around with all the cousins."

"Yeah, I do. But, in some ways, having Lonnie here was different." *I don't have to worry about these guys seducing you.*

"It's kind of lonely for me, being the only girl. Without Caroline, Victoria and Jessica, all I have are you guys."

He heard the loneliness in her voice, but he couldn't offer to be her best friend. That wouldn't work. So he only nodded.

When he finally escaped to the Pad, even the guys were wanting to know what was bothering him. After assuring them he was fine, he withdrew to his room and threw himself down on the bunk. He had to find some answers to his questions. Most specifically to the one question: What was he going to do...about Elizabeth?

He'd always told himself that while there was nothing illegal about their marrying, it would be frowned upon socially. And he didn't want to bring any shame to the Randall name.

True, but most of their neighbors knew the truth of their relationship. He didn't think they would be scandalized. Would his father think it was a bad idea? Why hadn't he ever asked him?

Because it was too great a risk.

That answer seemed to pop up out of nowhere and Toby lay there, contemplating it. Why? What was he risking?

Several things entered his mind, but he dismissed them. Finally, it came down to the greatest risk of all: losing his family.

It was always risky to pursue someone you love, to risk your heart. But if his family, and most especially Elizabeth, rejected his heart's desire, then he'd not only lose her but his family as well.

His beloved family.

Oh, his mom wouldn't refuse to speak to him. But coming home to the big family, arms wrapped around him, wouldn't be possible. It would be too awkward.

Chad and Megan would avoid him. Elizabeth would find other places to be when he came back. His male cousins would welcome him to the barn, feel pity for him, but he wouldn't be oldest cousin, world champion rodeo rider, someone to emulate and admire. He would be poor Toby.

Toby leaped to his feet and began pacing the room.

Was Elizabeth worth such a sacrifice? Especially when he had nothing to convince him she would welcome his advances?

After all, it wasn't like he could kiss her and see if she responded. If she slapped his face, he couldn't avoid her for a couple of weeks and it would blow over. He was her cousin!

He sighed and rubbed the back of his head. Had he stayed away from her for seven years hoping the feeling would fade? And what was this feeling, this wanting, that persisted without any encouragement

for so long? Chemistry? It certainly couldn't be constant contact. He'd stayed away.

And yet, the minute he'd seen her, felt her pressed
against him, her welcoming kisses on his face, it had
leaped out of control like a spark striking a brushfire.

All he had to do was kiss her, and he'd set another
brushfire of family response that would either burn
away the undergrowth that confused everything and
make a wonderful future possible, or set a flame that
would destroy his future as a Randall.

Looking out at the dark night, staring at the twin-
kling stars, Toby Randall faced a horrible truth.

He was a coward.

Chapter Twelve

Elizabeth sighed.

It was Saturday. Her free day. Her day to get caught up on chores. Her day to take stock of her situation and make plans for a new direction.

Her day without Toby.

He'd gotten a phone call yesterday demanding his presence in Denver today. He'd left before daylight so he'd be able to make the shoot to redo a magazine ad. So he wouldn't keep the gorgeous models waiting.

He was spending his day putting his arms around expensive supermodels, and she was sitting around moping.

That thought threw her into a frenzy of activity that by lunch had her laundry done, her room cleaned, the entire downstairs vacuumed. Her mother protested the vacuuming because several women came from town to do the basic cleaning every week, but Elizabeth had energy to burn.

At lunch she sat down with Red, Mildred, her mother Megan and Anna.

"Are you feeling all right, dear?" Megan asked.

"Yes, fine. Just a little restless."

"I guess this weekend is dull compared to going to Denver and seeing the rodeo," Red commented.

"I think it was the shopping more than the rodeo that caused the excitement," Anna said. "When I took the girls to Denver to shop for school, even Torie was excited. Jessica is always excited about shopping, even here, of course."

Of Elizabeth's two younger girl cousins, Jessica was very feminine. Torie was quieter, more studious. Elizabeth grinned. "I can believe that. And the stores in Denver are exciting, but I don't need to do any shopping for a while."

"Too bad," Red said. "'Cause you could've gone with Toby again today."

She'd thought about it. But she'd decided that it wouldn't be a good idea. She didn't want to become too obvious, tagging after Toby at every opportunity.

With the entire afternoon to get through, Elizabeth resorted to what she used to do when she had a problem. She decided to go for a ride.

An eagerness filled her. "I'm going to go for a ride."

Her mother protested, "But it's cool out today. And the weather's a little unsettled. Are you sure?"

"I'll check the weather before I head out, Mom. And I'll be sure I'm in early. I'll be in way before the guys. I just need a little fresh air."

Red and Mildred added several warnings that she

dutifully listened to, then she asked, "How about you, Aunt Anna? Don't you want to warn me, too?"

Anna chuckled. "No, Elizabeth. You probably know more about horse-riding than I do. But be careful."

"I will. I'm going to take old Buttercup. She'll keep me safe." The horse was a buckskin that had been retired a couple of years ago. Her gait was steady and to be trusted. And Elizabeth knew just where she wanted to go.

As kids, the cousins used to go camping over the first mountain pass, on the back side of a little mountain. She could take a snack and break her ride. She'd be able to think there.

"Red, could you fix me a snack?"

"You bet, honey. Cookies? An apple?"

"I think I'll be bad and have cookies, but I'll need something to drink. I'm going to change. I'll be back in a minute."

Half an hour later she was in the saddle, headed west. What a good idea. She drew in the clean air, filling her lungs. Not that the air was bad at the house. Not at all. But she had to share it with so many people. She loved her family. They were all supportive, loving. But there were so many of them. And she couldn't share her problems with them. They wouldn't understand.

She wasn't sure she did herself.

But she couldn't go on like this. Only happy when she was with Toby. Even then, when he was upset with her, she wasn't happy. Which didn't leave much time to be happy. On the hayride, the second half had been wonderful. She had ridden in Toby's embrace. She could've kissed his chin, or—or even his mouth. His lips were so tempting, so strong.

"I'm sounding like a teenager with raging hormones, Buttercup. Don't worry. I promise I'm older than that."

But lately she was beginning to wonder.

Fortunately Buttercup knew the path. Elizabeth only had to correct her a couple of times. Otherwise, she let her mind drift over her relationship with Toby…and what she was going to do.

She was almost to the point where they'd camped, a grassy area wedged between two rock formations. There were several trees. They'd always called it their fort.

She was smiling, thinking of those carefree days, when an antelope bolted from behind a nearby rock, startling both her and Buttercup.

Buttercup was frightened and reared. Normally Elizabeth could've handled her reaction, but she hadn't been paying attention, and she immediately tumbled off the horse. She landed wrong on her left foot and pain surged up her leg.

Worst of all, instead of calming down, Buttercup turned and ran…back up the mountain path toward the ranch.

TOBY CHECKED his watch. It was three o'clock. His foot pushed a little harder on the accelerator. He wasn't sure where his sense of urgency came from. He'd been away from the ranch more than he'd ever been there in the past few years. So it wasn't that he wasn't used to being away.

But for some reason, he felt a need to get home, to be sure everything was all right.

He released the tension with a sigh as he pulled to a stop by the house. His panic must be for nothing. Everything looked normal.

Then he caught a movement out of the corner of his eyes. He checked the area about the barn and saw old Buttercup. What was she doing out? Maybe she was looking for more food?

He got out of the truck and went to put her away. If the storm he'd heard about hit tonight, she'd be grateful for the protection of the barn.

When he got close enough to see that she was sad-dled, that tenseness returned. He checked her out for injuries and found none. Then he put her in the barn and headed for the house at a run.

When he got to the kitchen, no one was there. "Hello?" he called. "Where is everyone?"

Red stuck his head out of the bedroom off the kitchen. "We're restin', boy. Where's the fire?"

"Who went out riding?"

Red grew more serious. "Elizabeth, why?"

"Did she take Buttercup?"

"Said she was."

"Buttercup is back, still saddled, but no one with her."

"What?" came Mildred's voice, fear rising.

Red came into the kitchen, tucking his shirt into his jeans. "You think she's down, out there?"

"Has to be. I checked the barn. But Buttercup was outside the corral. Did she say where she was going?"

"Naw, but she promised to be back early," Red told him, looking at his watch. "'Bout now I reckon."

He passed Toby and crossed to the door leading to the hall. He opened it and called, "Megan? Hurry down." Then he turned to face Toby. "You going after her?"

"Yeah. I bet she went to our old camping place. She'd just have time to ride there and come back if she left around noon." Red nodded in confirmation. "There's a big storm coming in, carrying rain and sleet. Maybe snow further up. I won't have time to get her down that mountain before sunset, and it will be too dangerous after that, so pack for overnight."

"Right. You go get ready. I'll pack camping gear. You'll take a second horse?"

"Yeah."

Mildred rushed in as Toby headed for the back door, and he left Red to fill her in. Footsteps on the stairs meant Megan was about to burst into the kitchen and he didn't want to break the news to her.

Ten minutes later, he was back, long underwear under his jeans and shirt and a rain slicker on his arm. Red had a pile of gear on the floor, and Mildred was filling a canteen with water. Megan and Anna were cutting four thick roast beef sandwiches.

"You ate lunch, didn't you, boy?" Red asked.

"Actually, no, but—"

"Fix another sandwich," Red ordered.

"I don't have time, Red. I'll be all right."

"I'm not sending you out in a storm with no food in your belly." He nodded then relented slightly. "You can eat it while you're riding."

Toby knew it would save time to agree.

Anna started work on another sandwich while Megan came to him. "You'll bring her back safely, won't you?"

"Sure, Aunt Megan. You know I will." He leaned down and kissed her cheek. "It's just another camping trip."

"What if she's hurt?"

"I'll take care of her. I'm taking a first-aid kit. Quit worrying. I'm taking a radio with me, so I can let you know. Okay?"

He hoped he'd thought of everything. The only thing he didn't know for sure was where he would find Elizabeth. She was a good rider. Not one to lose her seat easily. And there'd been no marks on Buttercup.

If he found her at once, before the rain got too bad, everything would be okay. If she spent the night out on the mountain, unprotected, he couldn't make any guarantees.

"Could you get me a change of clothes for her?

It's supposed to rain and we don't want her catching a cold.''

Megan ran up the stairs at once.

''Start your sandwich while you're waiting on her,'' Anna suggested, pushing it in his direction.

That made sense, so he filled his hollow stomach with the sandwich, then started on his way.

Red went to the barn with him and loaded everything on the second horse while he saddled Cocoa. He took the food and put it on his own horse, just in case he and the second animal got separated.

''Be careful and bring her back safely,'' Red said, slapping Toby on his leg after he'd mounted.

''I will, Red. Thanks. I'll try to radio by the time the guys get in. Tell them to wait for my call.''

Red cleared his throat. ''Yeah. I will.''

Toby urged Cocoa out of the barn, the second horse following. He tied the lead rope around his saddle horn. He could already feel a change in the weather. Elizabeth would never have set out for a ride with it like this, but he suspected that at noon there'd been nothing to indicate a storm.

He set out at a steady lope, hoping to make as much time as possible while he was on level ground. Once they started up the mountain, he'd have to slow down.

And, please, God, let him find her.

ELIZABETH tried to curl her legs tighter to her body. She'd taken her jacket off and had it pulled over her head to serve as some sort of shelter from the rain. Her back was to a rock beside the trail.

Pain shot through her as she moved her ankle. She wasn't doing such a great job of keeping herself dry or warm.

She'd hoped Buttercup would go all the way back to the barn. It was her only hope for rescue. But it would have to be Red who came. The old man would have a hard time in this weather. And in another hour, no one would be able to get up that path in the dark, with it slick with rain.

That would be crazy.

And the men would only now be getting back from their day's work. Unless they'd taken a radio with them. She'd better start trying to figure out how to survive the night.

Up here, it was already getting below freezing at night. The only coat she had was drenched. It was a denim jacket with sheepskin lining. If the rain stopped soon, before it became too soggy, she might—who was she kidding? At best, she'd get through the night and have to go to the hospital for dehydration and frostbite.

She shrugged her shoulders. No sense crying over spilled milk. She was here now, alone, with no supplies. And she'd never kissed Toby.

That random thought almost made her laugh. But with the shivers that were coursing through her, she couldn't quite manage that. She was facing the trail that led back to the ranch. Back east. The rain was coming from the west.

Some small noise alerted her to movement. Concentrating her gaze, she thought she saw someone through the rain. Red! It must be Red.

She tried to rise up, but she only got to her knees. "Red!" she screamed.

The figure came to a halt, then started moving again.

Did that mean he'd seen her? She sank back into a heap against her rock and waited, straining to see through the rainfall.

If it was Red, he would have brought shelter of some kind, because he'd know they couldn't make it back down the mountain in the dark. But even better, if it was Red, she knew he'd bring food. Wonderful food. Her snack had gone with Buttercup. She'd had nothing since lunch, and it took a lot of energy to keep up all those shivers.

Fortunately, she was right beside the trail, so a couple of minutes later, she got to her knees again, ignoring the pain, when the rider got closer. The yellow slicker made it easier for her to see him in the gloom. "Red!" she called again.

The horses came to a halt and the man got down. "Not Red. It's Toby, if that's all right?"

Her eyes welled with tears at his response. "Yes! Yes, I'm so grateful. I didn't think anyone would be there but Red."

"You're hurt?" he asked, ignoring her response.

"My ankle," she replied, her voice filled with shame. She was a better rider than that.

He didn't touch her. Instead, he stepped past her, leading the two horses to the grassy patch. "I'll be right back," he called over his shoulder.

She sobbed, then chastised herself for her weakness. She might be miserable and frightened, but it hadn't been an easy ride for Toby. The least she could do was contain her misery.

In amazement, she watched him set up a one-man tent against one of the western rocks. He threw a pack in the tent after removing the canvas it was wrapped in to keep it dry.

Something dry. What a wonderful thought. Could he even build a fire? She couldn't move enough to get wood, even if she'd had a match. And she didn't.

He suddenly appeared beside her and scooped her up. "I'm going to put you in the tent. I want you to take off your wet clothes and get inside the sleeping bag. Throw them back out."

"Y-yes," she agreed, her teeth chattering.

"Do it fast. And be prepared cause I'm coming in after you as soon as I see to the horses. It's a two-man tent tonight."

She nodded, her voice caught in her throat. It was a small tent. But she'd share with Toby gladly. After all, he'd rescued her. But she would've anyway. She wouldn't be able to rest if he was out in the storm.

He strode quickly in the rain and the movement

jostled her swollen ankle. She buried her face in his neck and moaned.

He lowered her as he got on his knees. Then, with superb strength, he almost tossed her into the tent. Suddenly the rain wasn't falling on her anymore, and the grass beneath the tent floor was softer than the rocks she'd been sitting on.

"Stick your feet out so we can get your boots off," he ordered from outside. She did so, but she wasn't sure he would be able to get the left one off. The right one came off easily. The other one, as she'd suspected, wouldn't budge.

"Elizabeth, I'm cutting your boot off."

"No!" she protested, even though she knew she was being silly. This was no time to worry about losing a favorite pair of boots. It didn't matter. Toby ignored her. She felt his big knife slid down the side of her foot. Then, there was sudden relief to the pressure she'd been feeling on her ankle.

"Get your feet in before they get wet."

She did so and sat curled up in the tent. Relief flooded her.

"Are you undressing?" he called.

She'd forgotten his order. First she found the sleeping bag and rolled it out. Then she threw her coat toward the slight opening in the tent. Next came her jeans, difficult to maneuver since they were wet, especially when they had to pass over her ankle. After they were off, she removed her top and eased her feet into the warmth of the sleeping bag.

Just as she was zipping it up, Toby called, ''I'm coming in, Elizabeth.''

She scooted over as far as she could, which wasn't far. He came in anyway.

Fortunately he was mostly dry since he'd worn his rain slicker the entire time. Only his pant legs were wet. She expected him to fuss at her for taking up so much room. Or for being so dumb as to fall off her horse.

Instead, he pulled a radio out of the pack and punched some buttons.

''Red, I've got her.''

''Thanks be, boy. Here's her dad.''

''Toby? Is she all right?''

''She has a bad ankle. We're over the pass and it's too dangerous to try to get back in the dark. It's pouring rain here.''

''Yeah, we figured. Thanks, Toby. Can I talk to her?''

''Hi, Daddy,'' Elizabeth said as she leaned toward the speaker. ''I'm sorry.''

''What for?''

''For falling off Buttercup like a dude.''

''Accidents happen, little girl. You let Toby take care of you, and we'll be at the bottom of the mountain with a vehicle to bring you home as soon as it's daylight.''

''We'll be there about an hour after sunrise, Uncle Chad,'' Toby said. ''It'll take us that long to get down.'' They were picking up static and he signed off before anyone could say anything else.

"I feel like such an idiot!" Elizabeth exclaimed, her eyes tearing up again.

"Don't you start crying, Elizabeth," Toby warned with mock fierceness. "You know I have a weakness for tears. Maybe if I feed you. Will that take your mind off your misery?"

"Probably," she said with a sniff.

The pack he'd brought in was now at their feet and he struggled to get hold of it and tug it to him.

He pulled out two sandwiches and a thermos. "Red fixed decaf coffee. And I've got some pain pills that will help your ankle feel better."

Just as he'd efficiently put up their little tent, so he organized everything. He gave her a cup of coffee and two little white pills. After taking them, she enjoyed Red's delicious sandwich. Suddenly she felt much better. After Toby had eaten, too, he pulled the pack behind his back for support.

"Now," he said with a sigh, "you need to get some rest."

"But what about you?"

He slumped against the rock at his back through the tent and half lifted her so she was on top of his body. He spread his legs so she lay between. Then, with another sigh, this one she'd swear sounded like contentment, he wrapped his arms around her. "I'm comfy."

"But you don't have any cover," she protested.

"I have you. That'll do me. I have on long under-wear. Are you warm enough?"

"Mm-hmm, I'm doing great," she muttered as her eyes drifted closed. Those pills he'd given her must really be strong. She felt even better than she did when sleeping in her own bed.

Toby was there holding her.

RELIEF FLOODED the room as Chad clicked off the radio. Megan raced into his arms for a celebratory hug. Even Jim and Drew had tears in their eyes after learning of their sister's safety.

"Man, it's going to be a brutal night for those two. The weather report said it's going to be rough out-doors. We don't usually get a storm like this so early," Russ pointed out.

"He's well prepared," Red pointed out. "And Toby knows what he's doing."

"Yeah, he does, but I'm glad he found her before dark," Jake said. "How about some coffee, B.J.?" he asked his wife. The wives had offered coffee as they got in, but the emergency had kept them from accepting. Now everyone gathered around the table.

"We're going to owe Toby big-time," Chad said.

"Don't be silly, brother," Jake responded. "Toby won't look at it that you owe him." Before Chad could respond, the phone rang. Jake reached for it. "Hello?"

"Thanks for calling us. This storm took us by sur-prise." After a pause, he said, "Well, no, we're not all in. Toby and Elizabeth are out in the mountains. She fell off her horse."

"No, thanks, Griff. Toby prepared well, and he's got her safe until morning. We'll go get them then. Thanks for offering."

When he hung up, Chad said, "Nice of Griff."

"Yeah. He heard it's going to be a bad one. Figures to turn to snow about midnight."

"Why did Elizabeth feel the need to go off by herself?" Megan burst out.

"I figure it's 'cause all you galoots are men," Red said, gesturing to the cousins. "We need more girls around here."

"Hey, I'm not objecting," Rich said with a chuckle, "but let's have someone other than cousins."

His words got a chuckle from the other men, but B.J. said, "We should encourage Elizabeth to invite her friends out. Abby teaches with her. She went with her and Russ to Denver. We could invite Abby to spend a weekend."

"Yeah, great idea," Russ agreed with a lot of enthusiasm.

"For Elizabeth, son," Pete pointed out dryly. "Not for your benefit."

Russ avoided his father's gaze. "I was just trying to be friendly."

"We'll think of something," B.J. said with a smile. "But right now, we'd better get dinner ready. Someone's going to have to get up early to rescue our damsel and our hero."

Chapter Thirteen

Toby stared into the darkness of the tent. The rain had stopped several hours ago, but there was a whisper that told him it had changed to snow. A lot of snow.

Elizabeth shifted on top of him and he tightened his hold on her warm body. Where she lay against him, he was quite warm. Red-hot actually. But the outer edges of his arms, legs and back were cold. Not dangerously cold, but uncomfortably so.

Not that it mattered. He wasn't going to get much sleep that night anyway. His body was aroused from such close proximity to a half-naked Elizabeth, even though she was in a sleeping bag.

Then the hardness of his bed made his bones feel like brittle rocks. Every time he shifted, he creaked. But he had Elizabeth safe, here in his arms. That fact made his discomfort unimportant.

If she'd spent the night outdoors with no protection in this storm, she might have died. The world might go on without Elizabeth, but how could he? He dropped a kiss on her brow and laid his head against her soft curls.

Tomorrow, he was going to talk to his father about his feelings for Elizabeth. If Jake told him it was impossible, then he'd have to decide what he should do. He could afford his own place, start his training business and have a…a satisfying life. Yeah, sure.

But he had to take the chance. He couldn't walk away from Elizabeth without her knowing how he felt. How he would always feel. He had to try, no matter what it cost him.

With that decision made, he tried to settle again on his bed of nails and get a little sleep.

When he next opened his eyes, there seemed to be no change in their status. He was still holding Elizabeth in the dark. The whispering continued. When he managed to get his wristwatch close to his face, he discovered that it was almost seven o'clock.

He carefully slid Elizabeth off him to the floor of the tent. She settled with a groan or two, but she didn't wake up. He crawled to the tent opening where he'd left his rain slicker. The raindrops on it had changed to ice pellets, but the inside was dry.

He stepped through the opening into a snowy, bitterly cold world. He put on the slicker hurriedly and closed it, adding his hat for his protection. His gloves were in the pockets, so they were added to his uniform.

Next on the list were the animals. He'd spread blankets on both of them. Now he pulled out the two feed bags he'd brought and took care of their breakfasts.

All the while, he'd been thinking about the trip back down the mountain. He could leave all the supplies he'd brought and pick them up next week when the weather cleared up.

But it would be hard on Elizabeth to sit on a horse, especially with one foot exposed to the cold.

He slipped back into the tent and shook her. "Lizzie? Time to wake up."

She groaned, but didn't move. He leaned over and rubbed his lips over hers. It had been too tempting. And she wouldn't remember. Then he shook her again. "We've got to go, Lizzie. Your dad will be waiting."

He turned around and pulled out the spare clothes her mother had sent, a sweatshirt and warm-up pants. "Put these on."

"What?" she muttered, trying to open her eyes.

Sternly, he ordered, "We have to go. Get dressed. I even have some breakfast for you. You'll have to eat it cold, but it should help."

She was looking at him strangely, which made him nervous. "Come on."

She took the clothes from him and he dug out the other two sandwiches and a second thermos of coffee. He was grateful Red knew how to pack. The coffee, this time with lots of caffeine, was more important than even the sandwiches. Something hot in his body would get him down the mountain.

Another moan had him looking over his shoulder. Elizabeth had the sweatshirt in place, but she was apparently having difficulty with the pants. "What's wrong?"

"I—I can't get the pant leg over my ankle without—oh!" She gasped with pain.

He reached for the zip on the sleeping bag and ripped it down the side until he reached Elizabeth's foot. He eased the elastic holding the leg of the warmups over the swollen area, but after Elizabeth pulled them up, her cheeks red, Toby still saw a problem.

"Damn, that elastic is tight on your ankle, isn't it?"

She nodded, her expression full of misery.

He got out his knife again and sliced through the material and the elastic. The tension went away and it lay flat against her swollen ankle.

"Thanks," she whispered.

"Your mom may not thank me. I've just about ruined your wardrobe."

"B-b-but you saved me," she pointed out with a shiver.

"Get back inside the sleeping bag," he ordered. As she did so, he zipped it up, enclosing her in its warmth. "Your jacket is a piece of ice this morning. Even if it was wearable, your foot would be exposed to the weather."

"What are we going to do?" Elizabeth asked. She knew better than to try bravado, assuring Toby she could make it. They had all been taught as children to respect Mother Nature. ''Too bad I can't ride down the mountain in the sleeping bag,'' she said in an attempt at humor.

''That's what I was thinking,'' Toby said slowly. ''Yeah. I think that's what we'll do.''

''Wait a minute! I don't understand.''

''Don't worry, you will,'' Toby assured her with a grin. ''Let's eat so we can be on our way.''

They drank the coffee and hurriedly ate the sandwiches. Then Toby went out to get the horses ready. It was still snowing but the wind had died down. He was still debating exactly how he would get Elizabeth down the mountain. He could carry her in his arms while he rode Cocoa. He figured Cocoa could carry that much weight. He was a big gelding. But it was dangerous. Especially with the snow making the path tricky.

He decided the best way was for him to lead Cocoa down the mountain with Elizabeth on the horse's back, the other horse following. Once they got on the down side of the mountain, what wind there was wouldn't be a factor because the mountain would block it. That would help. And they'd be in the sunshine. Until later, no sunshine would reach this side of the mountain.

''Toby?''

He ducked his head back in the tent. ''Yes?''

''What should I do?''

''Just give me another minute.''

He loaded all the gear he was taking home on the

other horse. Then he returned to the tent. "I'm going to put you on Cocoa." He lifted her out of the tent.

"But I can't hold on," she protested.

"You've heard of ladies riding sidesaddle? Well, that's what you're going to do. Through the sleeping bag, I want you to hook your knee over the saddle horn. That will help stabilize you. Then hold on the best you can through the sleeping bag."

He set her in the saddle, then helped her arrange herself as he'd said. Zipping the sleeping bag to the very top, he lifted his Stetson off his head and settled it on Elizabeth's red curls. It was a little large, but it would protect her.

"Toby! You mustn't give me your hat! You take it. You'll get cold."

"I'll be moving. You won't." He ignored her continued protests and surveyed their little campsite. Everything was taken care of. He grabbed Cocoa's reins and turned him toward the trail. Over his shoulder, he said, "If you feel yourself slipping, yell!"

Then he started their return.

A half hour later, they'd crested the trail and looked down on the valley. Toby noticed there wasn't much sunshine since it was still snowing, but he thought he could see a vehicle at the base, which meant there was someone waiting for them.

He indicated that direction to Elizabeth, who was silent, but she gave a nod and a small smile. He suspected she was in a lot of pain, but he couldn't give her another pill. She wouldn't be able to stay on the horse.

"Are you doing all right?" he asked.

She nodded but said nothing. He patted her leg and went back to lead Cocoa. The horse was doing a good job on the trail. A couple of times he'd slipped a little but going down should be easier.

The trek down the east side was better, especially because the snow had stopped. He let the hood of his rain slicker fall back. Checking on Elizabeth, he got another small nod, no smile this time. He hoped Anna had come with the others. She was a nurse and would know what to do for Elizabeth.

When they were almost down, Chad and Jake joined them. They couldn't wait at the bottom with the others. There were two vehicles there, a pickup with a horse trailer behind it, and a Jeep Cherokee.

'You okay, son?" Jake asked as soon as he reached him, automatically reaching out to take the reins from his hands.

"I'm fine, Dad, a little tired, but fine."

Chad had gone to Elizabeth's side. "How are you, little girl?" he asked anxiously.

Jake stopped Cocoa so Chad could check on his daughter, and all three of them saw the tears form in her eyes. "I'm f-fine," she said with a gasp.

"She needs another pain pill, but I couldn't give her one or I wouldn't have been able to get her down the mountain. We need to get her to the bottom so she can get some relief,'' Toby said, hoping they'd take the hint and cut the greetings short.

"Right," Jake said, urging Cocoa forward once again.

Chad strode beside the horse, helping to steady Elizabeth and they reached the bottom a few minutes later. Anna and Megan were both there, waiting. Chad lifted Elizabeth from the horse and carried her to the Jeep Cherokee where she stretched out on the leather back seat. Megan tucked a pillow behind her shoulders as she comforted her.

"Anna?" Toby called. He held out the white pills he'd given Megan. "Here are the pain pills from the first-aid box I've been giving her. She hasn't had any this morning. If you'll give her some now, she'll soon be comfortable."

"Thanks, Toby. I will. Megan, where's the water?"

Toby knew Elizabeth was safe. Now he had to tend to his animals. He turned to discover Cocoa and the other horse being loaded into the trailer by his dad and Uncle Chad.

"Here, I can do that," he called.

"No problem," Jake assured him. "We've got them in. We'll unsaddle them when we get to the barn. You get in the cab. The heater should be running pretty well."

"I'm going with the girls," Chad called as he headed for the Jeep. Jake nodded and waved. He got behind the wheel of the truck and was putting on his seat belt when Chad appeared at the window and knocked. Jake rolled down the window.

"Here's Toby's hat. Elizabeth wanted to be sure he got it back," He grinned as he handed it through the window.

"Thanks," Toby said, reaching across to take it.

"I owe you, boy," Chad said, tears in his eyes. Then, before Toby could respond, Chad hurried back to the other vehicle.

"No! I—" Toby wasn't sure what he was going to say, but it seemed important to say something.

"Let it go, son. You did good. They *should* feel grateful."

Toby couldn't say anything. He wanted to explain that Elizabeth was his, his to save, to love, to protect. But he couldn't do that. Not yet. But he would talk to his dad and Uncle Chad soon. He would let them know what Elizabeth meant to him. Then he'd see.

IN SPITE OF all the loving care she was receiving, Elizabeth felt like an idiot. The doctor had insisted she remain in bed for twenty-four hours. Then she had to stay off her feet for three more days. She would miss three days of school.

It was almost impossible to find a substitute.

When she fretted about that, her mother promised to take her place until she could return.

"But your shop, Mom? What will you do?"

"Evelyn will work a few more hours. It's no big deal. I'll call her right now." Evelyn was a widow who worked in the antique and consignment shop Megan ran in Rawhide. "I might even hire another lady I've talked to for part-time work. I liked her, but I wasn't sure I'd have enough hours for her."

"I am going to get well. This isn't anything permanent, you know," Elizabeth pointed out. Her mother sounded as if she'd be in bed forever.

"Of course you are. Anna said you're doing very well."

Yes, she was, as long as she got a pain pill on a regular basis. Elizabeth sighed. "Are you sure Toby is all right? Have you actually seen him?"

"Of course I have. He was at the table last night for Sunday supper. And we embarrassed him to death by heaping praise on him. He's out working today. Did you want to see him?"

Elizabeth thought about that offer. "Yes, I would, when he can spare a minute. Just to be sure he's all right. He didn't even have any cover Saturday night because I was in the sleeping bag."

"And he let you wear his hat down the mountain. That was very gentlemanly of him."

"Yes." Elizabeth closed her eyes. "Mom!"

"Yes, dear?" Megan said, turning around. She'd been about to go downstairs.

"Mom, Toby's not really kin to me."

Megan stared at her daughter, not moving. "Well, he's not *blood* kin, dear, but he's part of our family."

"Yes, but—"

"Why is that important, Elizabeth?"

"Because I feel—different about Toby."

"Oh." Megan sat down on the side of the bed.

"Is that horrible?" Elizabeth whispered.

Megan reached out to take her daughter's hand. "No," she said slowly, "it's not horrible. But you were so recently engaged, it seems a little sudden."

Elizabeth's cheeks flamed. Her mother was only saying what everyone would think. "I've been in love with Toby forever. But he went away and didn't come back. I knew he wasn't interested in me. I tried to find some—some alternative. Sometimes I think that's why I was blinded to Cleve's faults. I was looking for someone the opposite of Toby so I wouldn't—"

"I was afraid of that," Megan said softly as she squeezed Elizabeth's hand.

"What do I do now?"

With a sigh, Megan stood and bent over to kiss Elizabeth's forehead. "I don't know, dear. But I'll talk to B.J. Maybe she'll have some idea. You need to take a nap now, and if you're very good, I'll try to induce Toby to visit you tonight."

With that, Elizabeth had to be content. Besides, it helped that someone understood her agony.

Megan left her daughter's room, a frown on her face. Poor Elizabeth. Many a girl had fallen for Toby. He wasn't cruel. He just didn't realize how he affected young women. Besides, Megan was sure he cared about Elizabeth.

As a cousin, or maybe even a little sister.

Since he'd come back this time, Megan had thought there was some tension between the two of them, but she'd figured it had something to do with readjustment.

She would be pleased if they married. She couldn't think of a finer son-in-law than Toby. What about Chad? It would be a little weird, but the more she thought about it, the more she thought it would be wonderful.

She'd heard B.J. come in from her appointments about an hour ago. She crossed to her and Jake's room and knocked on the door. "B.J.?"

After a second, B.J. swung open the door. "Hi, Meg. How's Elizabeth?"

"She's recovering nicely. But I need to talk to you."

"Sure. Shall we go down to the kitchen and have some coffee?"

Most of their conversations occurred there, but Megan couldn't guarantee privacy. "Why don't I fix us a tray of coffee and bring it up? That way we won't be interrupted."

B.J.'s eyes darkened as she nodded. Megan hurried away before she could ask any questions. She certainly didn't want to discuss the problem in the hallway.

Megan had fixed a tray, adding the pot of coffee, when Red came into the kitchen.

"You taking coffee up to the invalid?" he asked with a grin. "Here, let me add some cookies. I just baked them an hour ago. We want to keep our little Lizzie sweet.''

She started to correct him about the coffee's destination, but then she changed her mind. B.J. would like some cookies as much as Elizabeth.

Anna came in from outside, her nursing bag in hand, and Megan didn't hesitate to ask her to join them. She'd never had any sisters, but in the past twenty-five years, her sisters-in-law had easily filled that role. She added another cup and started up the stairs, Anna in her wake.

When she turned right instead of left at the top of the stairs, Anna called, ''Megan, what—''

She shushed her and knocked on B.J.'s door.

B.J. swung it open. Megan hurried in, as if afraid of being detected. ''Anna's here, too.''

Each couple had a sitting room linked to their bedroom. B.J. had two big sofas in front of the fireplace and a coffee table between them. Megan set the tray down. ''Red sent fresh-baked cookies, too.''

''Did he ask why we're having them here instead of in the kitchen?'' B.J. asked.

Megan looked guilty. ''No, because he thought I was taking the tray to Elizabeth's room.''

''Come sit down,'' B.J. invited the two of them. ''I'm dying to know what this is all about.''

Megan didn't know where to look. Or how to begin.

''Are you sure I should be here? I don't want to intrude,'' Anna said.

Megan leaned over and hugged her. "Oh, Anna, of course you should be here. I'd ask Janie to join us, but she's at her mom's. I need advice and y'all are the best friends I have."

"Is it Elizabeth?" B.J. asked.

"Sort of. And Toby."

B.J.'s spine straightened. "Toby? What's he got to do with anything? He saved Elizabeth. You said you were grateful."

"Of course I am—we are!" Megan exclaimed.

"He didn't do something wrong while he and Elizabeth—" B.J.'s eyes widened, a touch of fear in them. "I don't believe it!"

"No, B.J., no. It's not that he did anything wrong. But it—concerns him. You know, he's not *blood*-related to any of our children and—"

"You don't think he should inherit anything? Is that it? He's made his own way, Megan. He doesn't need—but the hurt—" There was hurt in B.J.'s face, too.

"No! No, I'm doing this all wrong. Anna, help me."

"Well, I would if I could, but I'm completely lost. Do you feel that Toby isn't a part of the family?"

"Of course not! He's as much a Randall as any of us. In fact, he's always been more a Randall than our kids because he works so hard at it. Don't you think that's why he's always achieved so much?" She saw B.J.'s face stiffen again. "I don't mean he's not as smart either. It's because he *is* as smart but keeps trying so much more than the others. If our kids would try as hard as Toby, there's no telling what they could do.''

B.J. had relaxed once again, a faint smile on her lips. "Now, I'm as confused as Anna. If Toby's not the problem, then what are we talking about?''

Megan tried again. "Elizabeth just broke her engagement.''

Anna and B.J. exchanged a look. Finally, Anna said, "We know.''

"Yes, well, I told her it was too soon, but I think maybe it's not. I'm not sure.''

"Too soon for what?'' B.J. asked, frustration rising.

"Well, that's what I'm trying to tell you.''

Anna chuckled. "But you've been trying for several minutes and we're still at a loss. Can't you just come right out and say it?''

"Yes, I can,'' Megan agreed. Then she stopped, braced herself, her hands clenched in her lap. "Elizabeth is in love with Toby!''

Chapter Fourteen

Toby waited until dinner was over before he approached his father and Uncle Chad. Quietly, he asked each of them to meet him in the barn.

As he turned away from his father to help with the cleanup, Megan touched him on the arm. "Toby? Elizabeth wondered if you could stop by her room this evening. She's worried about you."

"Worried about me?" he asked, confused. What was there to worry about?

"I think she's afraid you may have caught a cold."

"Why no, I haven't."

"I know, and I've told her, but she wants to be sure. Would you mind?"

He checked his watch. He could manage a quick visit before he went to the barn. Afterwards, who knew if he'd be able to face Elizabeth or not. "Sure. I'll run upstairs as soon as I finish here. Will she be able to get out of bed soon?"

"Tomorrow. And she can go back to work on Thursday," Megan assured him with a smile.

"Good. Tell her I'll be up in a second."

Russ, who must've overheard their conversation, said, "Go on up now. You're not so good at the dishes anyway and there are plenty of us."

Toby looked at the others. "Are you guys okay with that?" He didn't want his cousins thinking he was too good to wash up.

"Yeah," Rich agreed. "We'll excuse you for tonight. For Elizabeth's sake. Though why she needs to see your ugly mug I'll never know." Several of the young men laughed, but not Toby. He didn't know why Elizabeth wanted to see him, but he was glad of the opportunity to see her.

He missed her.

"Shall I just go on up?" he asked, feeling a little awkward about going to Elizabeth's bedroom.

"Sure. I'll come up with you and get her supper tray. If I don't, Red will get it and inspect the remains. Then he'll lecture her if she didn't finish it."

Toby grinned, knowing Megan was right.

After knocking on the door, Megan pushed it open and announced Toby's arrival.

When he entered behind her, he stared at a rosy-cheeked Elizabeth, dressed in a long-sleeved nightgown, in soft cream, her red curls on the pillow. He thought he'd never seen a more beautiful sight.

Clearing his throat, he said, "Well, you look a bit happier than the last time I saw you."

"So do you. Do you have a cold?"

"Nope, I'm fine." He walked a little closer to the bed.

She stretched out her hand, and he reluctantly took it, forcing himself to step closer. But it made him nervous. Elizabeth was always tempting. Elizabeth in a comfy bed could be overwhelming.

"I haven't thanked you," she whispered.

He looked at Megan, still in the room. "Um, I believe you did that night. Quite nicely. But you've forgotten because of the pain. So, that's all taken care of."

"I want to thank you again."

"Okay, you just did." His idea of a perfect thank-you would be to take her in his arms and kiss her. More than once. But he had a ways to go before that was a possibility. First he had to talk to his dad and Chad. Then, whether they approved or not, he knew he'd tell Elizabeth how he felt.

But then, he'd know whether he could offer her just himself, or the family they both loved.

Just thinking about it made him edgy. "I need to go." He pulled his hand free and took a step back.

"Why? Are you going to town?"

"No! But, uh, I want to talk to my dad about something."

"Training Buster? Is it going well?"

"Sure. Fine."

"How did Lonnie do in the Reno rodeo?"

His gaze intensified. "He did well. Why? Are you interested in him?"

Her eyes widened in innocence. "Only as your friend. I thought it would be polite to ask."

Toby chastised himself for his silly reaction. "Oh. Yeah, well, he did fine. Won some more points." He took another step back.

Megan had been straightening Elizabeth's room. Now she picked up the tray and said, "I'll go down now."

Toby immediately grabbed the opportunity to escape. "I'll go with you," he hurriedly said.

Elizabeth didn't say anything, but she looked sad. Damn, if she started crying, he'd fall to his knees beside the bed. That would be a disaster. He hurried to the door and held it for Megan.

"Toby?" Elizabeth called softly.

He looked over his shoulder, holding tightly to the door. "Yeah?"

"Thank you."

"No problem, sweetheart," he said in return and hurried out of the room.

Megan insisted on thanking him for visiting Elizabeth. He had to escape from her, too.

On the porch, he took a deep breath of mountain air and realized he'd just spent the easy part of the evening. Now he had to face Chad and Jake and explain why he was acting like a crazy man.

He checked his watch and realized they were probably already in the barn, waiting for him. He started down the path cleared of snow, trying to collect his thoughts. Easier said than done.

When he opened the door to the barn where old Buttercup spent her nights, Toby heard their voices. His dad and Uncle Chad were back in the tack room, probably working on gear that was broken. They never wasted time. Toby indulged himself by petting Buttercup, just long enough to gather his courage. Then he marched down the row of stables.

Their warm greeting when he appeared only reminded him again how much he'd be giving up if they didn't approve of what he wanted to do. But he had no choice. He wasn't going to give up Elizabeth.

"What's on your mind, Toby?" Jake asked. "Are you ready to go back to the rodeo?"

It had never occurred to Toby that his father would think that. "No, Dad! No, I don't want to go back to the rodeo. I'm happy here," he added.

Jake sighed with relief.

Toby felt such gratitude toward his father. Jake didn't want him to go, but he'd kept a smile on his lips when he'd asked that question. Jake was willing to let him go if that was what Toby wanted. What a father!

"I was hoping not," Jake said, "but I couldn't think of anything else it could be. Course I couldn't figure why Chad would be here and not the other two. We all rely on you, you know."

"Chad's here because—" Toby broke off. He couldn't quite get the words out. Then he drew a deep breath and squared his shoulders. "It's about Elizabeth."

Chad had been lolling on a bench, grinning at his oldest brother tying himself in knots. Suddenly he sat up straight, glaring at Toby. "What about Elizabeth?"

After all his worrying, his seeking the right words, the answer was painfully simple. "I'm in love with her." Once he got the words out, he leaned against the wall and waited.

"But she's your—" Chad began. Then he stopped, his mind obviously sorting through everything.

"But she's not," Jake said slowly, thinking, too. "Not by blood."

"What does she say?" Chad asked.

Toby's head came up. "She doesn't know."

Both men stared at him, stunned.

"How could I tell her? I'm her older cousin. I've protected her all her life. Now I become a—a predator?"

Jake cleared his throat. "I think you're getting a little dramatic there, Toby."

"I guess it is a little awkward," Chad added. "How long— I mean, is this sudden?"

"Since I came home from college," he muttered.

"That long? But you didn't say anything."

"She was a high-school senior, Dad. And I was a little stunned myself. I thought it would pass. But I couldn't stay here. So I went to the rodeo. It didn't pass."

"And you didn't come back until you heard she

was engaged,'' Jake added, his eyes narrowed as he stared at him. ''Did you come back to break it up?''

''No! I was happy for her…until I met Cleve. And I never said anything because I didn't think either of you would approve. So I tried to bury my feelings. I thought I could come back home because she wouldn't be living here anymore.'' He paused and took a turn around the room. ''But she's not engaged anymore and I'm going crazy. I have to talk to her, to tell her how I feel, but I realize it will make things awkward if she has no feelings for me. I'll…get my own place if—if she's not interested.''

''So we'll lose you again,'' Jake muttered.

''No, Dad. I won't go far away. And you and Mom can visit me instead of me coming over. We don't see Uncle Griff that much, but you talk on the phone. It won't be so bad.''

Jake embraced him.

''You two are acting like she's not interested,'' Chad said, pulling them apart. ''I think it's possible she is.''

Toby's heart leaped, then settled back to its regular beat. He wasn't sure Uncle Chad was that tuned to his daughter. After all, he'd thought she was going to elope when she'd decided to break up with Cleve.

''I just want to say,'' Chad continued, sticking out his hand toward Toby, ''that I'd be thrilled if she is. You'd be the best son-in-law in the world, Toby.''

Toby took Chad's hand and was pulled into another embrace. ''Uh, thanks, Uncle Chad.''

When he stepped back from Chad, he didn't know what to say. Finally, he said, "So, I'll find a time to talk to Elizabeth. Maybe after she's recovered."

"And I'll explain things to your mother," Jake added.

"And I'll talk to Meggie. I don't think she'll object."

"Our neighbors might talk. I mean, we were raised as cousins. Will that upset you?"

Jake grinned. "They did a lot of talking back when I was matchmaking. That doesn't matter."

"Your cousins may rib you a little," Chad warned with a grin.

"Yeah," Toby grinned back, knowing that for a certainty. But if it meant Elizabeth wanted him, that they could share a life together, he wouldn't mind. He began to actually think of a future with Elizabeth at his side, in his arms, and his father had to grab him to bring him back to the present.

"Son! Is there anything we can do to help?"

"No, I guess not. Just—just prepare the mothers."

"Don't worry," Jake said. "They always do what we want."

All three men laughed at that obvious untruth.

ELIZABETH didn't venture downstairs until midmorning. Her ankle still hurt, but she hopped most of the way down the stairs on one foot.

Her mother heard her coming and opened the door to the kitchen. "How does it feel?"

"Still sore, but I'm going without the pain pill this morning."

"Come on in and I'll fix you some breakfast," Megan said. She was the only one in the kitchen this morning. Red and Mildred had retired to their house across the yard. The men had taken some lunch with them and planned to be in early tonight. Megan had told the couple to take the day off until time to start dinner.

"Where's Red?"

"He and Mildred went home. I'm in charge of lunch."

"Is it just the two of us?" Elizabeth asked, wanting to be sure.

Megan nodded.

"Did you discuss my—my problem with Dad?" Elizabeth had wondered if her mother would, since they usually shared everything. That's the way a marriage should be, she thought.

That was the kind of marriage she wanted...with Toby.

"No, not last night. We got to bed late and he fell right asleep. Do you want me to talk to him?"

"I don't know. Did you talk to B.J.?"

Megan's cheeks brightened. "Uh, yes. I didn't do a good job of it, but I finally got it out."

"Was she upset?"

"Not when I finally explained. But before, she thought I was accusing Toby of something."

"What? But Toby hasn't done anything wrong! He wouldn't!"

Megan propped her hands on her hips. "Don't yell at me, young lady. I didn't accuse him of anything. B.J. just misunderstood. I straightened things out. Sort of."

The sound of a truck brought them both to an abrupt halt. Since Elizabeth couldn't get up, Megan crossed to the window. "It's B.J. She's back early."

B.J. entered a minute later, shedding her heavy coat and setting her vet's bag down by the door. "Brrr. It's still cold out there. How are you today, Lizzie?"

"Fine, Aunt B.J. I just got up, and Mom's fixing me a little breakfast."

Megan greeted her sister-in-law by bringing a cup of coffee to the table. "This will warm you up."

"Good. Red and Mildred okay?"

"Yes. I'm doing lunch today."

"Glad to hear it. It will give them a break," B.J. said with a smile, but she looked a little uneasy.

"Aunt B.J., I know Mom talked to you, but she was a little unclear about how you felt. I'd rather you be honest with me if you're against me and—and Toby trying—I mean—I know we're—"

"Perfect for each other?" B.J. asked, a relieved smile on her face.

"Do you really think so?" Elizabeth asked, a hopeful look in her eyes.

"Oh, yes. I've suspected before that you two

might—but you were a lot younger than him. Still are.''

''But I'm grown now.''

''Yes, and he waited for you. I kept wondering why he never showed any inclination to bring a girl home. Now I think I know.''

Megan put some toast in front of Elizabeth to go with her orange juice and looked at B.J. as she sat down. ''You think he's cared about her that long?''

''I'm not sure he knew why he didn't find a woman, but no one interested him. So when are you going to propose to him?'' B.J. asked, a teasing grin on her lips. ''I want grandbabies!''

''Me, too!'' Megan exclaimed. ''Oh, I hadn't even thought of that!''

''I had,'' B.J. said. ''If I have to wait for Caroline to finish med school and establish herself, I'll be eighty before I get any.''

''You and Toby will make the most wonderful babies,'' Megan said, a dreamy look on her face.

''And they'll have Randall blood,'' B.J. added softly.

A frown clouded Elizabeth's happiness. ''You don't think that's why—''

''No, not at all. Toby wouldn't agree to anything unless he loved you.''

''Well, he hasn't yet.'' Elizabeth had to keep reminding herself that she hadn't yet talked to Toby. ''Did you talk to Uncle Jake?''

''No, he came to bed late. And he was in the

strangest mood. I decided to wait until later, when the time is right. But I don't think he'll object."

"I didn't mean to pressure you. I probably can't get some time alone with Toby before the weekend anyway. He certainly didn't linger in my bedroom last night."

"Honey, it was awkward for him," Megan said.

"Yes," she agreed. "This whole thing is awkward."

"If—if I'm wrong, and he's not interested," B.J. began, "have you thought about afterwards?"

"I'm not going to drive him away, Aunt B.J., I promise," Elizabeth said seriously. "If I can't—manage, I'll find another job, a little farther away. We can't all live here together forever."

"But I don't want you to go away," Megan cried. "I just got you home again."

Elizabeth buried her face in her hands. All these conversations were making her crazy...and frightened. All she wanted was Toby. But what was it going to cost her? And her family.

SHE SPENT another day at home. Her ankle was causing her minor pain. She sat down frequently, propping it up to rest. But she also caught up on some lesson plans and organizing her closet.

Elizabeth waited anxiously for her mother's return so she could hear about all her students. Tomorrow she would see for herself.

Thinking about the children helped take her

thoughts off Toby and how she was going to approach him. She didn't hold out much hope. If he felt as she did, he would've done something about it. He wasn't one to hide from his feelings. He'd been good to her while they were on the mountain. She'd slept well that night, held in his arms.

But he hadn't made any moves that would've made her think he looked at her in any way but as a cousin.

A dumb cousin at that.

Except that fleeting memory. She wasn't even sure it was a memory. But she thought she remembered Toby's lips on hers just before she got her eyes open that morning. Was she dreaming? Probably. But she clung to that thought.

Wednesday night, after waiting all day to see him, Elizabeth was disappointed. He didn't come for supper. "Where's Toby?" she asked.

"He's working with Buster in the indoor arena. Said he was behind on the training. I told him I'd bring him some leftovers," Russ said, not stopping to gulp down his own food. "Is that okay, Red?"

"Sure, boy. Don't want any of you to go hungry."

"I could take it to him," Elizabeth suggested.

"Right!" Russ agreed with a derisive laugh. "That would be great. Hopalong Randall carrying a big plate of food on snow and ice. Talk about a disaster!"

Elizabeth reminded herself she'd find a time to pay Russ back for his teasing. She knew she shouldn't go out tonight, but the paths between the barns were clear. She didn't think she'd have a problem.

And she was going crazy.

She watched with longing as Russ loaded down a plate and left the kitchen. She started to ask him to let her go with him, but the cousins would get suspicious.

After the dishes were cleaned and order restored in the kitchen, she slowly climbed the stairs to her room. Once inside, she sat on the edge of the bed and stared at the wall. She'd already cleaned and organized everything. There was nothing on television except some silly sitcoms. What was she going to do until morning? Her babies at school were doing well, but they missed her, Megan said.

That was nice.

But she couldn't get her mind off Toby. She wanted something to happen. But she'd finally realized that mild flirting with Toby wasn't going to do it. Because of their peculiar circumstances, she would have to come right out and confront him. There would be no stages of dating. It was all or nothing.

Suddenly, she jumped to her feet, then winced as her ankle warned her not to be so impetuous. She exchanged her loafers for some pull-on snow boots. Than she checked her hair and makeup and brushed her teeth. A spritz of perfume, and she was ready.

She was going to end the torture she'd been suffering for the past few days. She could wait no longer. She was going to talk to Toby.

Even if she had to crawl on her hands and knees to get to that blasted barn!

She turned around and got some gloves.

Chapter Fifteen

"Everything okay at the house?" Toby asked between bites.

Russ had brought his food and settled down to visit while Toby ate. "Sure. Red fussed at us, as usual. The parents seemed to be in their own little world. Uncle Jake in particular was in a real good mood. And Elizabeth came down to dinner."

"She did? Is she all right?"

"Yeah. She's going back to school tomorrow. She thought she was so well recovered, she offered to bring your food to you."

Toby's heart clutched. He wished she had. No one else was working in the barn tonight. He could've been alone with her. He released a deep sigh. Bad plan. He wasn't in control right now. He'd been doing too much thinking about the future.

"I told her I didn't think that would be a good plan. She'd probably slip on the snow and ice and reinjure herself."

"You're probably right."

"Besides, who wants to talk to a girl cousin? They aren't much interested in things we're interested in."

"Unless, of course, it was Abby instead of a cousin," Toby pointed out innocently.

"You want to see Abby?" Russ demanded, panic in his voice.

"No, idiot, but I bet you'd choose Abby over one of your male cousins."

"Well, yeah," Russ said with relief. "But that's different."

"Yeah," Toby agreed with a rueful grin. "Have you got plans for the weekend?"

"Yeah. I see her every day I work in town. We're going out to dinner. Then I'm bringing her back to spend the weekend at the ranch. The parents think Elizabeth needs company, since we're all guys, remember?"

Toby chuckled again. "I hope you remember that when you get Abby here. You're going to want to spend all your time with her."

"I can't spend the night with her," Russ said with frustration.

"That serious?" Toby asked, watching him carefully. "You're being responsible, aren't you?"

"Sure, but it's not sex. I mean, I'm ready for sex with Abby, but I want to do everything with her, even sleep. I mean really sleep. I want to wake up with her."

"I'd say you've got it bad," Toby said, knowing exactly what he meant.

"Yeah. But I can't say much to Rich. He doesn't—I think he's afraid things won't be the same with us if Abby and I—do you know what I mean?"

"Yeah, but he'll adjust, Russ. It's probably hard on twins, but tell him how you feel."

"I guess I'd better. I wouldn't want to shock him."

The sound of the barn door opening drew both their attentions. "That's probably him now," Russ added.

But the person who emerged from the coat and hat wasn't Rich but Elizabeth. Toby set aside his plate of food and reached her side as she leaned against the wall, her sore ankle obvious.

"Elizabeth, what are you doing here?" he demanded.

"Well, thanks for the welcome," she said with irritation. "I was getting cabin fever. I thought I'd come watch you train Buster."

"Aunt Megan agreed to that? Risking you falling?" he asked incredulously as he scooped her into his arms and brought her to the bench he'd been sitting on.

He sat her down and reluctantly drew back.

"I didn't ask my mother if I could leave the house, Toby. I'm not four years old."

"I remember you went after your daddy when you were four. When she finally missed you, you were found in the pasture with Uncle Pete's rodeo bulls." Toby grinned at the memory.

"A long memory isn't such a wonderful thing,

Toby Randall. I may be able to think of a few stories about you, too,'' Elizabeth warned.

Russ settled back down on the bench. "Hey, I haven't heard stories like this. You got a good one on Toby?'' he asked, glee in his voice.

"Never mind, Elizabeth. We'll call it quits on tales.'' Toby didn't think she knew any stories, but the parents could've passed some on.

"Shoot, I think she should tell me something good,'' Russ said. "You've always been the perfect child, Toby. When we came along, all we heard was 'Toby wouldn't do that,' ''

Toby shrugged. "I've had my share of bad behavior, Russ. You guys are just as good as me, and you know it.'' He'd fought this problem before. "In fact, I may disrupt the family in the near future, and you and Rich would become the picture of perfection to hold up to the rest of them.''

Russ laughed. "Yeah, right. What are you going to do? Return to the rodeo and win some more belt buckles? That would really upset everyone.''

He stood and stretched. "Ready to go back to the house now, Elizabeth? I'll help you back.''

"No!'' she exclaimed, startling her cousin. "No, I want to see Toby work with Buster. I'll stay a while.''

Toby stared at her. Then he turned to Russ. "Thanks for bringing down the dinner, Russ. I'll make sure Elizabeth gets back to the house before her bedtime.''

Russ shrugged and headed for the door. "Okay.

I'm tired. I need to call Abby, then I'll hit the sack. See you tomorrow."

Toby watched Russ go, knowing that he'd be left alone with Elizabeth. Anticipation built in him.

"Is he serious about Abby?"

Toby turned to stare at Elizabeth again. "What?"

"I just wondered if he talked to you about Abby. She's—she's in love with him. I want her to be happy," Elizabeth said. She dropped her gaze from his eyes. "It's sad when you love someone and he— he doesn't love you back."

"You ever suffered from that?" he asked, trying to keep his voice casual.

She turned her face away. "I—when I was younger," she mumbled.

"You had a crush on Mr. Sanders?" he teased, hoping for more information. Mr. Sanders had been the local chemistry teacher at the high school, almost to retirement when Toby had gone to school.

"No! No, not Mr. Sanders."

"Then who?"

She got up from the bench and hobbled over to the corral. "Aren't you going to start training Buster? Where is he?"

"I took him back to the stall so he could eat a little while I was having dinner. I'll go get him."

ELIZABETH drew a deep breath as she watched Toby stride toward the stalls at the far end of the arena. She should've just told him she'd had a crush on him. But the moment had slipped by.

Now Toby would be in the corral with Buster, and she could watch him with no problem. She loved watching him work with animals. He was so gentle, yet firm. He had a natural grace that made him a pleasure to watch, even if she weren't in love with him.

She settled back with a smile as he led the horse into the arena.

An hour later, Toby led Buster over to the corral fence near her. "I'm calling it a night. He's too tired to learn much more. Wait here and I'll help you back to the house."

She smiled at him and nodded. But as he led the horse back to the other end, she stood and circled the outside of the corral. After all, she limped a little, but it wasn't too painful. She'd help Toby rub down Buster.

By the time she had negotiated the length of the arena and reached the stalls, Toby had almost finished with Buster.

"Need any help?" she asked softly.

Both the cowboy and the horse jumped. "Hell! You scared us both to death, Elizabeth. I expected you to wait for me."

She stared at her handsome cowboy and decided she wouldn't ever have a better opening than that. "I've *been* waiting for you, Toby. All my life." Her body began trembling as she watched him stare at her.

"What did you say?" he asked, his gaze intense.

She swallowed her nervousness. If he rejected her, at least she'd know. "I said, I've been waiting for you all my life."

After standing like a statue, Toby abruptly gave Buster several more swipes with the brush, then put the brush away. He came out of the stall and carefully latched the door.

Elizabeth watched his methodical movements in growing irritation. Wasn't he even going to answer her? Maybe that was his response. He didn't feel the same as her so he would just ignore what she'd said. She started to turn away, but a hand on her shoulder stopped her.

"What do you mean, Elizabeth?"

"Are you sure you want to know?" she asked, edging closer to his tall, strong body.

His arms came around her, removing the space between them. "I want to know."

She took a deep breath. "I'm in love with you, Toby."

As if she'd lit the fuse to a Roman candle, her world exploded. Toby's lips covered hers for that long-desired kiss that more than met her expectations. Her body was on fire everywhere they touched, but it wasn't enough. She wanted to be skin to skin, heart to heart. Her fingers found the top snap on his shirt and began unfastening it at once.

His mouth continued to lay waste to any thoughts she could put together. When he finally raised his head, she thought she'd die, as if he provided her oxygen by his lips.

She pulled his head back to her mouth. He'd been kissing her neck, but she needed his mouth on hers. By that time, his chest was exposed to her seeking fingers and she ran her hands over his muscles, the sensation of silky hair beneath her fingers spurring her on.

"Lizzie..." he managed to get out, over the sound of his thundering heart. But she refused to let him start a conversation now. Talk wasn't what she wanted.

And why had she never known how exciting sex could be? She'd never been with a man who tempted her. But Toby drove her crazy.

She made no demur when Toby began stripping off her shirt. In fact, she did what she could to help him as long as it didn't keep her from touching him. The sooner they were naked, the sooner she'd be completely happy. She was totally consumed with the experience. She wanted to be one with Toby for the rest of her life.

TOBY KNEW he was losing control. It had been so long since he'd had any sexual encounters that he wasn't surprised. But he'd never experienced such surges, such uncontrollable desires.

Something kept nudging his brain, but his body was so in charge at the moment he couldn't figure out what he was supposed to remember. He wanted Elizabeth naked and beneath him. He'd attack anything or anyone that kept him from reaching that goal. He did remember to move them into an empty stall so they'd have some straw for cushioning and some privacy.

At one point he pulled back. "Lizzie, are you sure?"

When she grabbed his neck to draw him back down, he gave up any attempt to think. All he could do was feel, and it felt like heaven.

There was one other point when he paused, a teaching so emphatic, so drilled in, that he thought of protection. But he loved Elizabeth, had plans for their future, and that precaution was easily dismissed. The force that drove him was so strong, he couldn't stop.

When he finally got her jeans and panties far enough down her legs that he could enter her, he stopped removing things and turned to seduction. He stroked her and teased her with his fingers. Elizabeth responded with an eagerness that only increased his own ardor. However, when he entered her and felt the initial resistance, he realized what it was that he was supposed to remember.

She was a virgin.

Toby halted. He was about to deflower the love of his life? He was going to hurt her? Her first time would be half-dressed in a horse stall? He tried to pull back, to harness all that power driving him.

"Toby!" Elizabeth almost screamed. "Don't stop. Don't stop now. I can't—I need—"

He did, too. Her cries made it impossible for him to pull back. He plunged past the obstacle and almost ended his dream prematurely. But he tried to take care of Elizabeth, to show her how incredible loving her could be. Slowly he began the age-old rhythm, barely hanging on until he felt her joining in, becoming lost in the sensations. When he felt the beginning of her release, he finally gave in to his own pleasure...and it was monumental.

He lay on top of her, stunned by the flow of happiness, by the sudden exhaustion after such a rapid surge of energy. He wasn't sure he could move, much less walk.

"Toby?" Elizabeth whispered.

He froze. He expected anger, pain, retribution.

"That was—absolutely incredible. Is it like that all the time?"

He laid his forehead on hers, his eyes closed, and gave thanks he hadn't disgusted her. Opening his eyes, he stared down at her flushed face. "I can't tell you that, sweetheart. It's never been that incredible for me. Until now with you."

He realized they had a lot to talk about and rolled off her, afraid he would hurt her if he remained on top of her. "Uh, we need to talk," he muttered as he stood, pulling up his underwear and jeans.

Elizabeth smiled up at him, lying there in disarray, not showing any shame or need for modesty, which pleased Toby. He didn't want either of those things to ruin her first experience. He was distracted by that thought. He was her only lover. Pride filled him. A ridiculous pride, he told himself, but it was there, like it or not.

He smiled at her and then frowned. She hadn't begun to cover herself, and his body started to react...again. He couldn't possibly—but his body was telling him he could. He stepped out of the stall. "Put on your clothes," he ordered over his shoulder. How could he talk to her when he wanted her so soon again?

And they had to talk. Now. First of all, they wouldn't be able to talk in the house. The only place would be Elizabeth's room. And the parents would want to know what was going on. She couldn't go to the Pad, either. His cousins would be shocked. So the barn was their only opportunity.

The most important decision to make was when they would be married. The sooner the better, especially since he didn't think he'd be able to work a bed into their courtship and the hay was definitely not his favorite. Too scratchy.

Maybe the mothers could manage a small wedding by the weekend. He stood there in a daze, picturing himself on his honeymoon with Elizabeth, far away from the family he loved. He did love them, but he loved Elizabeth more.

"Toby? What's wrong?"

The lazy, sated tones she'd used earlier were gone. Elizabeth sounded upset.

He spun around, ready to take her in his arms

again, if she was dressed. Undressed, it would be too tempting. To his relief, she was buttoning the last button on her blouse and he reached out for her arms.

"Anyone in here?" a voice boomed from the arena.

Toby's voice caught in his throat. The timing was exquisite. Five minutes earlier and they'd both have been horribly embarrassed. "Yeah! Back here."

It sounded like the manager, Jeff Hardy, who'd worked on the ranch most of Toby's life. Toby took Elizabeth's arm and pulled her after him, going to the front of the barn.

"Oh, hi, Toby, Elizabeth. I saw the lights on as I was going to the house and thought I'd check," Jeff said, grinning at them.

"I was working on training Buster, and Elizabeth decided to keep me company," Toby explained, keeping his voice relaxed "We just finished putting him away."

"Oh, good, so you're going back to the house? I have to talk to your dad about one of the men, and I'd like your opinion, too, Toby, if you don't mind."

Jeff took his agreement for granted and headed for the door to the barn where the light switches were. Toby had no choice but to follow him, shrugging into his jacket as he went. When he realized Elizabeth was limping rather badly, he stopped.

"Lizzie? Does your ankle hurt more?"

"I can't—can't keep up," she said, her voice breathless.

Jeff stopped, too. "I forgot about your injury, Elizabeth. You shouldn't have come this far from the house."

Toby found himself hoping they could let Jeff go ahead and at least settle a few things before he took Elizabeth back. But Jeff had other ideas.

"As soon as we get outside, Toby, we can make a seat between us with our arms and have her back home in no time."

Jeff opened the door of the barn, then reached back and flicked the switches for all the lights over the arena.

In the dark, Toby dropped a kiss on Elizabeth's neck and helped her through the dark to the outside. The wind had mostly died down, but it was still cold out there.

"Your coat?" he asked Elizabeth. "Did you forget your coat?"

"Yes, but don't worry about it. I'll get it tomorrow, or you can get it. Let's just hurry to the house," Elizabeth said.

Toby wanted to protest. Another reason for them to stay by themselves gone away. Jeff offered his arms in the folded position to connect with his and make a seat for Elizabeth.

"We'd better hurry, then, or she'll be a popsicle," Jeff teased.

Toby joined his arms with Jeff's and Elizabeth slid onto their makeshift seat. Feeling her bottom against his arms, her right hand around his neck, didn't help

Toby forget what had just happened in the barn. He hoped he didn't become too aroused before they reached the house.

Once they reached the back porch, Elizabeth got down and opened the back door.

Several of the parents were having a cup of coffee around the table when they came in. Megan, Elizabeth's mother, reacted first.

"Elizabeth? I thought you'd gone up to bed. Where have you been?" She leaped to her feet and came to her daughter.

"I went to the barn to watch Toby training Buster. The horse is really doing well," she added.

"But you could've fallen and hurt yourself even more. That was not a wise choice, honey."

Jake had stood up and acknowledged Jeff's arrival while Megan was fussing over Elizabeth. When he learned the reason for his visit, he suggested he call all his brothers to the office, and then included Toby also.

With Megan and now Anna surrounding her, Toby knew he wasn't going to get an opportunity to talk to Elizabeth tonight. Nor would he be able to do so in the morning. So it appeared they'd have to try for the barn tomorrow evening. He hoped Elizabeth understood.

She headed for her bedroom, escorted by the women, leaving a lingering look over her shoulder, one that raised his blood pressure again. He remembered his visit the other night, how delectable she'd looked in the bed. He wished he were visiting her tonight. But he couldn't bed her, here in his father's house, without having married her.

With a sigh, he followed the men to his father's office.

An hour later, a decision having been made about the cowboy in question, Jeff excused himself to return to his home. The men stood and began to file out of the office, but Jake stopped Toby. Then he stopped Chad, too.

"We'll be out in a minute, guys," he added for Brett and Pete, who stared at them, wondering what was going on.

Toby was afraid he knew. Damn, he wasn't ready—he felt so guilty for what he'd done tonight. He didn't want to—

"Toby, did you and Elizabeth talk tonight?" Jake asked after the door had closed.

"Uh," he stalled and then cleared his throat. "Sort of."

"What does that mean?" Chad asked, eagerly leaning forward in his chair.

"She cares about me." That much he could say for sure. It suddenly occurred to him that he hadn't said those words to her. Damn! What did she think? Surely she knew he loved her or he wouldn't have—didn't she?

"Toby," Jake repeated several times to draw him from his thoughts.

"Yes, Dad?"

"I know this is highly personal, but can't you tell us a little more than that?"

Toby stared at him, panicked. Finally, he blurted out the one thing he'd intended to keep to himself. "It was her first time...and we made love."

He felt so guilty about her first experience. He should've remembered before he— But once she touched him, he'd lost all control.

"You what?" Chad roared.

"Look, Uncle Chad, I hadn't—I loved her for a long time. To finally have the right to—I mean, she wanted—it was a mutual thing, I promise. We love each other. We're going to be married. I didn't plan tonight. But we were alone and—and it just happened."

His father got up from behind the desk and circled it to lay a hand on Toby's shoulder. "Okay, son, we understand."

"You do?" Toby asked, astounded by his father's response.

"Yeah. Don't we, Chad?"

To Toby's amazement, under Jake's stare, Chad's cheeks flushed and he nodded his head. "Yeah, we understand."

Toby was overwhelmed. He fell into his chair and covered his face with his hands.

"She's okay?" Chad asked, sitting down himself.

"Yeah, but we didn't get a chance to really talk."

"Have you set a wedding date?" Jake asked.

"No. But I want it to be soon. I can't handle a long engagement."

"Okay, don't worry. We're a big enough family to get it done right away. With us helping you, you have nothing to worry about," Jake assured him.

Chad nodded. "Yep. We'll help."

Chapter Sixteen

When Elizabeth's alarm went off the next morning, she opened her eyes, aware that something was different. Then she remembered. She'd made love with Toby last night...for the first time.

It wasn't dreams that had changed her. It was real, the time she'd spent in Toby's arms. As she stretched, her body announced a few muscles that ached. She'd taken a hot shower last night, but it hadn't erased the changes she felt in her body.

Last night, she'd had trouble going to sleep. Her body had wanted to relive the glorious event. Her mind had worried. She'd told Toby she loved him. His answer had been to make love to her. Not to say "I love you, too." Did that mean he loved her? Or did that mean he was attracted to her?

She had a lot of questions for Mr. Toby Randall today. But first she had to go teach her babies. Impatience filled her. She should at least be able to talk to him this morning, but the breakfast table wasn't where she wanted to have such an important conversation.

Especially not with her cousins looking on.

She hurried through her preparation for school, hoping to get down a little early in case Toby came in alone. Maybe he was anxious to talk to her, too.

She hoped so. She wanted a future with Toby as her lover, her partner, her…everything.

She'd just finished twisting her hair into one long braid down her back when she heard a little knock on her door. Curious, she swung it open. "Mom? What is it? I'm not late, I know."

Megan slipped into her room and closed the door behind her before she turned and hugged Elizabeth.

"Of course you're not late. I just wanted to congratulate you or whatever you do to a bride! My baby!" she exclaimed, sniffing a little. "I'm so glad everything worked out. I was afraid—I mean, it's such a relief that Toby feels the same as you. We're going to manage everything. All you have to do is get time off for your honeymoon, and then be the prettiest bride in the world. Oh! I'm so excited!" She hugged Elizabeth again and then left the room.

Elizabeth stood there, unable to say anything, even after her mother left. Then, gradually, she began to sizzle, heat rising in her until she let out a scream of frustration.

What had just happened? Someone had told her mother not only that she had talked to Toby, but that they had agreed to marry. Her heart clutched. What if that someone had told her even more, had explained what they'd done last night?

She'd kill him.

Not only had Toby—it had to be him—told her mother something *she* would never have told her, but he thought he could get out of a proposal? That their marriage would be an assumption? That she'd never have a marriage proposal to tell her children about?

Well, Mr. Toby Randall could think again!

He'd been there when Lonnie thought he could wait until Friday night to ask her out. Hadn't he learned anything?

Fury burned through her. She grabbed her papers and work material, stuffed them into the cloth bag she used, and stomped out of her bedroom and down the stairs.

The men were entering the kitchen from the back porch as she reached the swinging door. She stiffened her shoulders, glared at all of them and set down her belongings. Then she moved to the cabinets to gather the dishes and silverware to set the table.

"Sorry I'm late, Mildred," she murmured. "Mom stopped by to talk to me."

"No problem. Is everything all right?" Mildred asked.

Elizabeth stopped, turned to glare at Toby again. Then, in a loud voice, to ensure that he heard, she said, "No. Everything's not all right."

She'd gotten his attention. He rushed across the room. "Lizzie, what—"

She sailed past him, her nose in the air. Putting the plates down, she then began sorting the silverware, giving each person a fair share.

"Lizzie," Toby whispered over her shoulder. "We'll talk this afternoon."

Again she stopped and turn to stare at him. "Will we?"

"Of course. We can't—"

"What are you guys whispering about?" Casey asked as he sat down at the table, which, of course, made sure everyone noticed.

Elizabeth didn't bother answering. After all, it was Toby who was doing the whispering.

"Uh," Toby said, then stopped. "I'm not sure. Elizabeth seems upset."

"Seems mad to me," Rich said, puzzlement in his voice.

"You're right, Rich. I *am* mad. Sometimes people assume things without asking the proper questions. And sometimes, they even tell people things when they shouldn't!"

She went to the stove to grab two platters filled with eggs, bacon and sausage. Red gave her a questioning look. He didn't say anything, but he followed her to the table.

"Any of you boys upsetting Elizabeth had better straighten things out," he warned. "Before you eat," he added and glared at all of them.

Toby got out of his chair. "That would be me. Come on, Lizzie," he muttered and grabbed her by the arm. He pulled her in the direction of the spare bedroom behind the kitchen where Red and Mildred sometimes took naps.

Elizabeth didn't fight him. She was ready to clear things up.

Once they were in the room and the door closed, she changed her mind about talking. Throwing her arms around his neck, she raised her lips for a kiss. Fortunately for Toby, he didn't try to resist but took what was offered.

Several minutes later, he broke off the kiss, hoping he could control himself. After all, there was a bed just behind him. His breathing heavy, he said, "We'd better do some talking unless you want to be late for school."

"You mean you're not all talked out? From what I gathered, you've already done a considerable amount of talking," she pointed out.

Toby knew he was in trouble then. "What happened?"

"My mother came to my room this morning. She's so pleased we're marrying. The family will get everything ready for the wedding. I don't have to worry."

Toby groaned. "Sweetheart, I didn't intend— Our dads trapped me and—I felt so guilty, I accidently confessed before I could—"

"You what? You told them?"

"Yeah, but only to reassure them that I was marrying you," he hurriedly said, thinking his words would make everything better.

"How do you know?"

That question stopped him. He stared at her. "What do you mean? You said you loved me." He knew she'd said those words. He'd treasured them, thought them, dreamed them.

She didn't say anything. Staring at him, she seemed to be waiting for something.

Then, placing her hands on her hips, she said softly, "I do love you, Toby Randall, but if you think that gives you the right to *assume* I'll marry you, even though you didn't bother telling me you love me, or bother to propose to me, you've got another think coming. I will not face my children and tell them you didn't propose to me. I won't!" she finished, stamping her foot, like a two-year-old throwing a temper tantrum.

Then she was gone.

Toby, finally understanding what was wrong, tried to gather his thoughts, to figure out how to right the wrong before he went back into the kitchen. When he finally gave up and went after her, she wasn't there.

"Where's Elizabeth?" he demanded.

Red glared at him. "You didn't do a good job of apologizing. She ran out of here, tears in her eyes, without any breakfast! And she forgot her lunch, too. Now she's going to be hungry all day!"

"What did you do, Toby?" Russ asked.

It was clear to Toby that he had a lot of apologizing

to do. And not just to Elizabeth. His cousins were thinking he was pretty lousy, too.

He squared his shoulders. "I made a mistake."

He was so involved in figuring out what to say that he hadn't heard the parents coming down the stairs. They entered as he'd started his confession.

"What's going on?" Jake asked.

Red answered. "He's telling us why sweet Elizabeth is so mad at him and left without eating."

Toby released a big sigh. "You all might as well know. Lizzie and I are in love." He held up a hand as several people started to speak. "I know we're cousins, but we're not really. We have no common blood. And we've—I've loved her for a long time. Last night we finally realized that—we love each other.

He hated to explain his situation, but he had no choice, so he continued. "I assumed we would be married, but we couldn't talk it out last night. I said something to, uh, someone else, who apparently told Aunt Megan. She greeted Elizabeth this morning, chattering about the wedding."

"Oh, dear, I'm so sorry," Megan said. "I was so excited, I couldn't wait— Oh, dear. Was she upset?"

"She said she wasn't going to marry me," Toby said.

It seemed everyone had an opinion about that. It was Jake who brought them under control. With a roar, he silenced everyone. Then he said to Toby, "Surely she doesn't mean it?"

"I hope not. But if she marries me, it will only be because I make a spectacular proposal that she can tell our kids about." Several smiles appeared, including the one on Toby's lips. Just thinking about having children with Elizabeth brought pleasure.

"Cool!" Casey said into the sudden silence. "So will their children be my nieces and nephews?"

"Probably more second cousins," B.J. said.

"What are you going to do, son?" Jake asked.

"I don't know. But I'm open to suggestions."

Everyone gathered around the table.

By NOON, Elizabeth was a nervous wreck. She loved Toby with all her heart. She was thrilled he wanted to marry her. But she was mad that he hadn't bothered to ask her.

Given that, she thought she'd done the right thing. But what if he didn't think so? What if he didn't ask her? He could return to the rodeo or get his own place. He could date the most beautiful women in the world. He could forget all about her.

And she'd die of a broken heart, all because he took her for granted.

She was pacing the teachers' lounge, wringing her hands, when Abby came in. "Hi, Elizabeth, how's—what's wrong?"

"Oh, Abby!" Elizabeth exclaimed and ran to her friend for a hug and a shoulder to cry on.

"Elizabeth?" Abby hugged her willingly. She even

patted her back to help with the tears. But she wanted to know what was going on.

"I may have ruined everything!" Elizabeth exclaimed. "Toby told everyone we were getting married, and I chewed him out for not asking me. I told him I wouldn't!" she finished, more tears falling.

Abby didn't say anything until Elizabeth stopped crying.

"I think I need to sit down and have a soda," she said, "so you can explain a few gaps in that story."

"Gaps?" Elizabeth asked, catching her breath.

"Yeah, like when did the two of you realize—I mean I know you had decided—but what about Toby?"

"Last night. We talked—well, we didn't talk. But I told him I loved him."

Abby gasped. "You are so courageous! That must've been tough."

Elizabeth nodded.

"And does he love you?"

"I don't know. He didn't bother to say." Renewed anger stiffened Elizabeth's back and she sat down at the table, folding her arms over her chest.

"But what did he say? He had to have said something when you blasted him with that fact."

"No, he didn't. He just m-made love to me," Elizabeth confessed, keeping her gaze on the table.

"Elizabeth!" Abby stared at her with wide eyes. "You mean you and Toby—you did?"

Elizabeth nodded but still didn't look at Abby.

"But how was it? I mean, I've had sex once before, but I wasn't impressed. With Russ it feels—I mean I think I want to, but I'm not sure."

"It was incredible," Elizabeth whispered.

"This is wonderful! Do I get to be in your wedding?" Abby asked with a laugh.

"I turned him down, Abby. He may never ask again."

ELIZABETH had just ushered her children out of the classroom that afternoon when the school secretary made an announcement over the sound system. "Miss Gaylord, come to the office for a phone call, please."

It was unusual for the office to announce a phone call. It usually meant the call was something urgent. In spite of her mental state, worried to death over her own life, Elizabeth hoped Abby didn't have an emergency to deal with.

By the time she'd straightened her room in preparation for the next day and gathered up the things she needed to take home with her, the school was quiet. When Abby popped her head in the door, it startled Elizabeth.

"Oh! Is everything all right? I heard them call you," she said, gesturing to the speaker.

"Oh, yes, everything's great. It was Russ. He wanted me to catch a ride with you out to the ranch instead of bringing my own car. You don't mind, do you? We'll have to go by my apartment to get my bag."

"No. That will be fine. I'm in no hurry." In fact, she was dreading going to the ranch. Facing Toby tonight was going to be even harder than last night. "I thought you were going out with Russ."

"We are, but we're going to Buffalo to dinner. Coming here to get me would just make for extra driving. I hope you don't mind that I'm spending the weekend there."

"No, of course not. Are you ready?"

"Come to my room. I'll gather my stuff and then we'll go." Abby led the way back to her room and kept up a steady stream of chatter as she loaded papers into her bag.

Elizabeth sat down and scarcely heard anything Abby said. Her mind was on Toby.

"Ready?" Abby said, standing at the door with a smile.

Elizabeth jumped up and apologized for keeping Abby waiting. They walked out to warm weather.

"I can't believe how much the weather has changed in just a few days. Snow last weekend and now it's almost balmy."

Abby talked about the weather like it was of the utmost importance. Elizabeth nodded.

"Do you want me to drive? You seem a little distracted," Abby pointed out.

"No, I'll drive."

At Abby's apartment, it seemed to take her friend forever to gather her belongings.

"I thought you'd already packed," Elizabeth finally said after twenty minutes of Abby wandering her apartment.

"I did, but I want to look extra good tonight for Russ. He's the sweetest guy."

"You don't think he's too young? He's your age, you know." Elizabeth liked Toby being older than her. As if it mattered, she reminded herself with a sob.

"Elizabeth, don't worry. I'm sure everything will work out. I can't imagine Toby making love to you and then walking away. That's not how he would operate."

"He might if I told him to get lost," Elizabeth said with a sniff. "Besides, it's so awkward with no one knowing, like we're sneaking around or doing something to be ashamed of. I don't know if we'll ever be able—I mean, people will talk."

"Does it matter?"

"Not to me, not if I can have a life with Toby, but I don't want him to be ashamed of me."

Abby gave her a gentle smile, then looked at her watch. "I think it's time to go."

Elizabeth frowned. "Do you have a schedule? I don't think the men will even be in yet."

"Russ is. Remember, he called me?"

"Oh, yeah. I wonder why he's in early." Elizabeth stood and headed for the door. Would Toby already be in, too? If she went to the arena to get her coat from last night, would he be there working Buster?

Did she have enough courage to face him?

Abby chattered all the way to the ranch. When Elizabeth said something about the road being unusually crowded, Abby claimed it was probably a sale they hadn't read about. Maybe one of the nearby ranchers was selling off his herd.

"We would've heard about that," Elizabeth said, frowning. She grew even more intense when they reached the dirt road to the ranch house and discovered all those unexpected cars were turning there, too. "What's going on?"

"I guess we'll find out when we get there." Abby's lack of concern puzzled Elizabeth almost as much as the cars. Why would she sound that way unless she knew what was going on?

"What did Russ tell you?" she suddenly asked, catching Abby off guard.

Abby almost jumped in the car seat, and her cheeks heated up. "What? I—I told you. He wanted me to ride with you so he wouldn't have to go back into town to pick me up before we went to dinner."

She'd topped the little hill that looked down on the house, and it had the appearance of a big-city parking lot. There were as many cars there as people in Rawhide. Something strange was going on. "What else?" she demanded of her friend.

"Um, that's about it."

"Abby, you'd tell me if—if someone died, wouldn't you?" Elizabeth suddenly asked, her voice trembling.

"Of course I would. It's not that, Elizabeth, I promise. Everyone is fine."

"Then why is half the state of Wyoming in my backyard?"

TOBY STOOD on the dance floor their cowboys had constructed that afternoon in the indoor arena. He couldn't believe they'd finished it in time. The tables set up near the stalls were covered with dishes of food. Red and Mildred, with some of the mothers helping, had cooked all day. Then the neighbors, all invited by phone this morning, had brought their own contributions.

They were giving Elizabeth a surprise engagement party.

It had been his mother's idea. B.J. had said he should make sure Elizabeth knew he wasn't ashamed of what they were doing. It had never occurred to him that Elizabeth would even think such a thing, but the phone calls this morning got kind of complicated, explaining things. So he was glad that was out of the way.

He was glad Russ had come up with a way for Abby to accompany Elizabeth. That way he could be sure she'd get there—and not run away at the last minute.

Casey, having been sent outside to be the lookout, dashed into the barn. "She's coming!" he shouted at the top of his voice.

Toby cleared his throat, ready to do his part. Ready,

willing and eager to do what he should've done before.

With Abby at her back, pushing her, Elizabeth stumbled into the barn amid a roar of applause and shouting. She came to an abrupt halt, just inside the door and stared in shock.

Toby walked over and took her hand. Then he turned and led her toward the center of the arena, on the stage that would serve as a dance floor tonight.

As soon as they were in the center, he held up his free hand to the crowd. They fell silent as he turned to face Elizabeth.

"Elizabeth, almost all our friends and neighbors, and most of our family, came here to be witnesses to what I'm about to say. I didn't want anyone to doubt my sincerity or my enthusiasm."

Her eyes were as wide as could be, their beautiful blue standing out from her fair skin. Had he overdone it? But he wanted a good story for his children, hell, his grandchildren, too.

He dropped to one knee, keeping her hand in his. "Elizabeth Randall, will you marry me, and be my wife for the rest of our natural days?"

She smiled, and he waited for her agreement. Instead, however, she asked a question. "Why?"

Damn, he'd forgotten something after all. "Because I love you with all my heart and soul."

Tears glistened in her eyes as the crowd stopped breathing to hear her answer.

"Yes, Toby, I'll marry you," she said clearly.

Then she collapsed into his arms and he swung her around in a circle, giving thanks that he'd been patient and waited for the love of his life.

He set her down again and kissed her, a long, deep kiss that held all those promises he'd willingly make. The crowd of well-wishers screamed and cheered, but he ignored them as he made sure Elizabeth had no doubts about how he felt about her.

Then he whispered in her ear. "I don't want to jump the gun again, but could you manage to be ready for the wedding next Saturday? The parents assured me it could be done."

With all the noise, he wasn't sure he could've heard her answer anyway, so it was a good thing she nodded. He held up his hand and the crowd quieted again.

"I hope you good folks can stand another party real soon, because you're all invited to the wedding…next Saturday at high noon, right here."

The cheering began again. But added to it was the sound of a couple of fiddles and a saxophone. Toby pulled Elizabeth into his arms, tucking her up against him, and began a slow waltz around the floor, suddenly questioning the wisdom of so many witnesses. There was no way he and Elizabeth would get any time alone tonight.

Probably not for the next week, he reminded himself. But after that, he'd have her to himself for the rest of his life.

"My thoughts exactly," Elizabeth whispered in his ear, then added a kiss.

He was in real trouble if she could read his mind. But he'd manage, he decided. Yes indeed, because he thought he was beginning to read hers, too.

THE NEXT SATURDAY dawned bright and golden, a perfect fall day in Wyoming. Toby had been warned at breakfast, minus Elizabeth, to stay out of the house until time for the wedding. He wasn't allowed to see the bride until he met her at the temporary altar in the arena barn.

Since he'd had a few minutes alone with Elizabeth last night, enough to cuddle her and add a few steamy kisses, he figured he could make it that long. But after the wedding, they had a car picking them up and driving them to Casper, where they'd take a short flight to Denver. Their ultimate destination was Hawaii. But their wedding night would be in Denver.

They'd stay in Hawaii for two weeks. That should be long enough to adjust to being married. They might even get a tan—if they made it out of the bedroom every once in a while. He wasn't promising anything.

The entire family was here, the five cousins in from college. In spite of only having a week, the parents had been right. They'd had enough time to make a wedding to remember.

"Hey, cuz, you haven't given me the ring yet," Russ reminded him.

"No, I haven't. And you won't get it until we're at the altar, and you can't pretend to lose it."

"Aw, Toby, it was just going to be a little joke," Russ protested. "We have to do something to you for your wedding day."

"Yeah," Rich added. "You wouldn't let us have a bachelor party." He rubbed his hands together with relish. "We had great plans."

"Yeah, I figured. But you'd better be glad I was on to you. Now, when it's your turn," he particularly looked at Russ, "I won't be trying to pay any old debts."

Rich didn't look too concerned, but Russ frowned and looked away. Toby figured he'd be married within six months. If he could wait that long. Toby was just glad his waiting was over.

He dressed in his tux, as did his cousins, and they all walked to the arena.

"Have you seen her dress?" he asked them. He'd been worried that she wouldn't be able to find what she wanted, but she'd assured him she had.

They all shook their heads. The barn was already filling up with their friends and neighbors. On a table in the back was a huge mound of presents. Toby was grateful because he wanted Elizabeth to experience everything, but he didn't care about gifts. He was getting Elizabeth.

When the music finally began, he drew a deep breath and waited for his bride to enter.

Elizabeth stood outside the door to the barn, her hand tucked into her father's arm.

"You okay, little girl?" Chad asked gruffly.

She suspected he was fighting back tears.

"I'm okay, Daddy," she said, reaching up to kiss his cheek.

"I'd ask you if you wanted to change your mind, but I don't think that's a possibility. I see the same look in Toby's eyes as I had in mine. I wouldn't give you to anyone who didn't look at you that way."

"I hope my marriage is as good as yours, Dad."

"Me, too," he agreed, looking into the barn, trying to catch a glimpse of Megan. "Me, too."

Abby and her cousins had all gone into the barn, their dresses varying shades of blue, each progressively darker until Abby's dress, which was a royal blue.

Then the wedding march began, and Elizabeth and her father stepped forward. Her gaze was fixed on the tall, handsome man in a tux, standing before the altar at the end of the dance floor, so everyone could see.

Her childhood dream that had grown and strengthened through the years was finally coming true. She and Toby would share their love and be together for the rest of their lives.

Toby's eyes glowed as she came closer, and he eagerly stepped forward to take her hand from Chad. Her nerves disappeared. She was in Toby's hands now. There was no other place for her, for the rest of her life.

THE PARTY was almost over. The bride and groom were off on their honeymoon. Only a few diehards were still dancing, a few hearty eaters still picking at the tables of food, or nibbling on their pieces of wedding cake.

Jake sat in a folding chair, looking at everything. "It's hard to believe, isn't it?"

B.J., her head on his shoulder, understood at once what he meant. "Yes, it is."

"You mean our kids getting married?" Chad asked. He and Megan, Anna and Brett and Pete and Janie were all there, too.

"I guess," Jake agreed. "Just that we've managed so well. When I first hired Megan and those two other women, I had a vague hope that things would work out, but we've been incredibly lucky."

"Yeah," Pete agreed with a lazy grin. "No one's laughing at you now, Jake."

"Nope, they're not. And there's only one thing that could top off my happiness."

Everyone sat up and stared at him.

"You're not happy?" B.J. demanded.

"Sure, I'm happy. But we need babies. We need to secure the next generation."

Megan immediately protested. "I think Toby and Elizabeth need some time to themselves, Jake. I don't want any pressure put on them to have children at once."

"No pressure," Jake assured her. "It's just a thought. Besides, it doesn't have to be them. We have lots of kids around here. And pairing them up should be as easy as shooting fish in a barrel."

"Jake Randall, behave yourself," B.J. ordered. "There's no need to matchmake for this generation. They'll manage just fine."

"Of course not," Janie agreed. "After all, they don't have the famous Chloe fear of matrimony to overcome."

"Right," Anna agreed softly.

"We'll see," Jake said, exchanging looks with his three brothers. "We'll see."

There's a baby on the way!

HARLEQUIN®

AMERICAN *Romance*®

is proud to announce the birth of

AMERICAN *Baby*

Unexpected arrivals lead to the sweetest of surprises in this brand-new promotion celebrating the love only a baby can bring!

Don't miss any of these heartwarming tales:

SURPRISE, DOC! YOU'RE A DADDY! (HAR #889)
Jacqueline Diamond September 2001

BABY BY THE BOOK (HAR #893)
Kara Lennox October 2001

THE BABY IN THE BACKSEAT (HAR #897)
Mollie Molay November 2001

Available wherever Harlequin books are sold.

HARLEQUIN®
Makes any time special®

Visit us at www.eHarlequin.com   HARBABY

Harlequin truly does make any time special. . . . This year we are celebrating weddings in style!

A Walk Down the Aisle
WEDDING CELEBRATION

To help us celebrate, we want you to tell us how wearing the Harlequin wedding gown will make your wedding day special. As the grand prize, Harlequin will offer one lucky bride the chance to **"Walk Down the Aisle" in the Harlequin wedding gown!**

There's more...

For her honeymoon, she and her groom will spend five nights at the **Hyatt Regency Maui.** As part of this five-night honeymoon at the hotel renowned for its romantic attractions, the couple will enjoy a candlelit dinner for two in Swan Court, a sunset sail on the hotel's catamaran, and duet spa treatments.

A HYATT RESORT AND SPA

Maui • Molokai • Lanai

To enter, please write, in, 250 words or less, how wearing the Harlequin wedding gown will make your wedding day special. The entry will be judged based on its emotionally compelling nature, its originality and creativity, and its sincerity. This contest is open to Canadian and U.S. residents only and to those who are 18 years of age and older. There is no purchase necessary to enter. Void where prohibited. See further contest rules attached. Please send your entry to:

Walk Down the Aisle Contest

In Canada	In U.S.A.
P.O. Box 637	P.O. Box 9076
Fort Erie, Ontario	3010 Walden Ave.
L2A 5X3	Buffalo, NY 14269-9076

You can also enter by visiting www.eHarlequin.com
Win the Harlequin wedding gown and the vacation of a lifetime!
The deadline for entries is October 1, 2001.

HARLEQUIN®
Makes any time special ®

PHWDACONT1

HARLEQUIN WALK DOWN THE AISLE TO MAUI CONTEST 1197
OFFICIAL RULES
NO PURCHASE NECESSARY TO ENTER

1. To enter, follow directions published in the offer to which you are responding. Contest begins April 2, 2001, and ends on October 1, 2001. Method of entry may vary. Mailed entries must be postmarked by October 1, 2001, and received by October 8, 2001.

2. Contest entry may be, at times, presented via the Internet, but will be restricted solely to residents of certain geographic areas that are disclosed on the Web site. To enter via the Internet, if permissible, access the Harlequin Web site (www.eHarlequin.com) and follow the directions displayed online. Online entries must be received by 11:59 p.m. E.S.T. on October 1, 2001.

   In lieu of submitting an entry online, enter by mail by hand-printing (or typing) on an 8½" x 11" plain piece of paper, your name, address (including zip code), Contest number/name and in 250 words or fewer, why winning a Harlequin wedding dress would make your wedding day special. Mail via first-class mail to: Harlequin Walk Down the Aisle Contest 1197, (in the U.S.) P.O. Box 9076, 3010 Walden Avenue, Buffalo, NY 14269-9076, (in Canada) P.O. Box 637, Fort Erie, Ontario L2A 5X3, Canada.

   Limit one entry per person, household address and e-mail address. Online and/or mailed entries received from persons residing in geographic areas in which Internet entry is not permissible will be disqualified.

3. Contests will be judged by a panel of members of the Harlequin editorial, marketing and public relations staff based on the following criteria:

   - Originality and Creativity—50%
   - Emotionally Compelling—25%
   - Sincerity—25%

   In the event of a tie, duplicate prizes will be awarded. Decisions of the judges are final.

4. All entries become the property of Torstar Corp. and will not be returned. No responsibility is assumed for lost, late, illegible, incomplete, inaccurate, nondelivered or misdirected mail or misdirected e-mail, for technical, hardware or software failures of any kind, lost or unavailable network connections, or failed, incomplete, garbled or delayed computer transmission or any human error which may occur in the receipt or processing of the entries in this Contest.

5. Contest open only to residents of the U.S. (except Puerto Rico) and Canada, who are 18 years of age or older, and is void wherever prohibited by law; all applicable laws and regulations apply. Any litigation within the Province of Quebec respecting the conduct or organization of a publicity contest may be submitted to the Régie des alcools, des courses et des jeux for a ruling. Any litigation respecting the awarding of a prize may be submitted to the Régie des alcools, des courses et des jeux only for the purpose of helping the parties reach a settlement. Employees and immediate family members of Torstar Corp. and D. L. Blair, Inc., their affiliates, subsidiaries and all other agencies, entities and persons connected with the use, marketing or conduct of this Contest are not eligible to enter. Taxes on prizes are the sole responsibility of winners. Acceptance of any prize offered constitutes permission to use winner's name, photograph or other likeness for the purposes of advertising, trade and promotion on behalf of Torstar Corp., its affiliates and subsidiaries without further compensation to the winner, unless prohibited by law.

6. Winners will be determined no later than November 15, 2001, and will be notified by mail. Winners will be required to sign and return an Affidavit of Eligibility form within 15 days after winner notification. Noncompliance within that time period may result in disqualification and an alternative winner may be selected. Winners of trip must execute a Release of Liability prior to ticketing and must possess required travel documents (e.g. passport, photo ID) where applicable. Trip must be completed by November 2002. No substitution of prize permitted by winner. Torstar Corp. and D. L. Blair, Inc., their parents, affiliates, and subsidiaries are not responsible for errors in printing or electronic presentation of Contest, entries and/or game pieces. In the event of printing or other errors which may result in unintended prize values or duplication of prizes, all affected game pieces or entries shall be null and void. If for any reason the Internet portion of the Contest is not capable of running as planned, including infection by computer virus, bugs, tampering, unauthorized intervention, fraud, technical failures, or any other causes beyond the control of Torstar Corp. which corrupt or affect the administration, secrecy, fairness, integrity or proper conduct of the Contest, Torstar Corp. reserves the right, at its sole discretion, to disqualify any individual who tampers with the entry process and to cancel, terminate, modify or suspend the Contest or the Internet portion thereof. In the event of a dispute regarding an online entry, the entry will be deemed submitted by the authorized holder of the e-mail account submitted at the time of entry. Authorized account holder is defined as the natural person who is assigned to an e-mail address by an Internet access provider, online service provider or other organization that is responsible for arranging e-mail address for the domain associated with the submitted e-mail address. **Purchase or acceptance of a product offer does not improve your chances of winning.**

7. Prizes: (1) Grand Prize—A Harlequin wedding dress (approximate retail value: $3,500) and a 5-night/6-day honeymoon trip to Maui, HI, including round-trip air transportation provided by Maui Visitors Bureau from Los Angeles International Airport (winner is responsible for transportation to and from Los Angeles International Airport) and a Harlequin Romance Package, including hotel accomodations (double occupancy) at the Hyatt Regency Maui Resort and Spa, dinner for (2) two at Swan Court, a sunset sail on Kiele V and a spa treatment for the winner (approximate retail value: $4,000); (5) Five runner-up prizes of a $1000 gift certificate to selected retail outlets to be determined by Sponsor (retail value $1000 ea.). Prizes consist of only those items listed as part of the prize. Limit one prize per person. All prizes are valued in U.S. currency.

8. For a list of winners (available after December 17, 2001) send a self-addressed, stamped envelope to: Harlequin Walk Down the Aisle Contest 1197 Winners, P.O. Box 4200 Blair, NE 68009-4200 or you may access the www.eHarlequin.com Web site through January 15, 2002.

Contest sponsored by Torstar Corp., P.O. Box 9042, Buffalo, NY 14269-9042, U.S.A.

PHWDACONT2

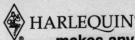